A TOWERING
TRUMPETER

Kevin Clarke

For my awesome wife, Debra

ACKNOWLEDGEMENTS

I was inspired by Timothy Findley's novel "Not Wanted On The Voyage" when I was considering how to craft this tale. Sincere thanks to a brilliant storyteller.

This story would not have been possible without the encouragement of my friend Denise Newton. Her advice to "go all the way out there" when writing a satire made it a very fun experience indeed. Many thanks Denise!

Hearty thanks go out to my cousin and fellow author Zoe Sutton Harris for the editing advice and cheering me on. I owe a debt of gratitude to Gary Carr for his insightful advice and pointed questions about my early manuscript. Also, a tip of my hat goes to the Cyrus13 team and pixelatedpeach at Fiverr. Many thanks for your valuable input. I am deeply indebited to Kristina Stanley for providing the editing tool Fictionary. Without it this story would not be what it is.

Thanks, above all, to my wife Debra for listening to all the silliness of every version of the tale and song lyrics through its one-and-a-half years of development.

CONTENTS

PREFACE

Amos Moses knew there was more to him than anyone gave him credit for, and he was bound and determined to prove it. After learning the ropes of the business world from his evil father, and the game of life from his conniving older brother, he manages to wrest control of the family business from his old man.

He promptly sets out to correct his obvious physical defects in hopes of fulfilling his quest for adoration. Having successfully transformed his personal image and his business empire into a branding juggernaut, he leads his right-wing base of supporters in a fight for freedom, but primarily for idolization, against the socialist President of The Great Union of Territories.

All The Stuff's Been Spoken
(Bob Dylan - Everything Is Broken)

♫ *Spoken lies...by a spoken King*
Spoken Dems...with spoken stings
Spoken rifles...by spoken reds
Folks are tweeting...in spoken threads
They're all fightin
Some are croakin
Cause of what's been spoken ♫
♫ *Spoken fossils...with spoken hates*
Spoken kisses... with spoken baits
Spoken militias...against spoken states
All we hear is...hate filled debates
Spoken from mouths that should never be opened
Too many things were spoken ♫
He can deceive ya, even after the race
The rage increases, all around his base
♫ *Spoken nutters...with spoken cause*
Spoken knuckles...on spoken jaws
Spoken lobbies...throwin spoken stones
Spoken choices...in vile tones
He's like Macbeth, don't dare go provokin
Anything he's spoken ♫
So when he spoke and they marched downtown
Now the Capitol is a burnin down
♫ *Spoken demands...they're spoken proud*
Spoken graffiti...spoken aloud
Spoken gripes...by a spoken fool
Ain't no mending...his spoken fuel
First he was towering, now he's chokin
On allllll the lies he's spoken ♫

Chapter 1 – Who Ya Gonna Call?

The bell rang for class as Amos was fumbling to get his books and close his locker. He cringed when he heard one of his fellow students, Cruisin Ted they called him, shout out, 'Hey, googly boy! Where are you going?'

Amos knew he couldn't run; he'd pay for it later if he did. He turned around to face the music and said, 'To math clathth.'

'You mean math *class*, hahaha,' Ted laughed. 'Well, here's a numbers question for you. What's worse than getting a poke in one of your wandering eyes?'

Amos shuffled his feet and scratched his baldish head. 'I dunno, what?'

Ted lunged at his face with two outstretched fingers and when Amos recoiled, he tripped over his feet and fell to the floor.

Ted stood over him laughing and sneered, 'Getting poked in both of them.'

Amos picked himself up and fumed, just like every other time. He looked down the corridor, which was empty, and thought, 'At least nobody saw that.'

The stupid little pranks they pulled on him were bad enough, but the ones that humiliated him publicly were the worst. Like the time when two of Ted's best friends, Marc-*Oh!* and Dandy Rand-ee distracted him while he was contemplating not much of anything over his lunch in the cafeteria. That rotten so-and-so Ted had snuck under the table and tied his shoelaces together. When Amos got up to leave, tray and all, including himself, crashed to the floor in front of everyone.

Yes, they were the ones who really rotted his socks. Cruisin Ted, Marc-*Oh!*, and Dandy Rand-ee. But still in all, he didn't hate school, just the bullies who were in it. Most of the other students liked him, but they just didn't want to be seen hanging out with a geek like him. As for the mean ones, well, there was no end to the ridicule of his lisp and the way he looked. When they made sport of his wandering eyes (yes, both of them) it was more than he could take, than *anyone* could take. To him there were only two solutions; hide under his bed for the rest of his life or get revenge.

The next morning, his elder brother Abe was at the kitchen table eating a goose egg for breakfast when Amos walked in, wanting some advice, or at least a shoulder to cry on. Abe watched Amos grab a bowl of black-eyed peas from the fridge and heat them up on the stove. Amos had a cloudy look on his face when he slammed the bowl down on the table and sat down across from him.

Abe asked, 'What's twistin up yer testies today, little spittler?'

'Oh, Abe. I'z in a dark plathe, black ath black kin be,' Amos said.

Abe never even saw it coming before it hit him, a little black speck of pea landed on his left eyelid. He picked it off, inspected it, and said, 'Zat sumpin ya might call ironic? Anywho, tell me just how dark it is, sweet pea-shooter.'

Amos laid out his woes to Abe, 'There ith a lot more to me than thothe boneheadth at thchool ever thought about, but I don't know how much more I can take of their harraththment. I know I might look like the goofietht guy what wuz ever born, and talk that way too, but I ith gonna prove to em one day they croththed the wrong fella. And now they're callin me The Wanderer, yeah, The Wanderer, arrgh! I *hate* that name, not to thay I didn't like the tune. Anywho, I'm tellin ya, one of thethe dayth I'll get even with em and have em eatin outta the palm of me hand, mayhapth even have em bowin down to me all adorin-like!'

Abe offered in support, 'Look Amos, ye *is* differnt, and that's what kin set people off to greatness. Take superstars like David Bowie, Tiny Tim, or even Marilyn Manson. They wuz awesome, leaders of the pack, willing to lay it all out there and push the envelope. But it will only happen if you embrace it. You know, go with what you've got, or more to the point, love the one yer with.'

'I ain't catchin yer drift, Abe,' Amos said.

'I mean turn what looks like a negative into a positive. And it starts with lovin yerself, little brother.'

'But Abe, how do I do that?'

'Just leave it to me, Amos, and I'll learn ya how to go about that. And remember this, I've got your back and I ferever will. Just hang with me and I'll get ya'll squared away. And fer the time bein I'll set those apes to rights in a jiffy, okay?'

Amos shrugged his shoulders and said, 'Okay Abe, thankth brother.'

A few days later when Amos got home from school he went out on the back deck to find Abe relaxing in a lounger. Abe broke out into a broad grin when he saw Amos and then winked, 'Member what I told ya the other day, dear brother? I'd always have yer back, right!'

Amos had a quizzical look on his face when he said, 'Yeah, I'll never forget *that*, Abe.'

Abe pulled out a lipstick-red ballcap from behind him and said, 'Then let's get started on makin somethin out o ye.' He gave Amos the hat and said, 'This'll soften yer image a tad and it's got a nice emblem on the front.'

Amos inspected the crest on the hat and smiled when he read out what it said - "MAGA", and underneath read (Make Amos Glorious, Amen!).

Abe pointed out, 'I got a big box o em delivered yesterday, so ye'll never run out.'

Amos donned the cap and thanked Abe profusely, but it didn't help all that much at school. It just gave the bullies something to tear off his head and taunt him with. They had backed off on their pranks to some degree since Abe had threatened them, but he remained a target of their jokes and scorn.

And there were no sports teams for Amos to impress the girls with, no siree. Not like Abe, who was a master at it all. Quarterback, Power Forward, Striker. Hot chicks dripping off him all the time, with Amos right beside him, looking for some sympathy loving. And he did get to second base now and again, which, from what he gathered, was more than his fellow classmates were getting.

All the extracurricular activities didn't leave Abe much time to hit the books, but he didn't need that kind of education. He was learning every day, in every game. The game of life, to him, was where it happened. And the lesson he took from it was - go with the offence and have some dependable shmucks behind you to close off the rear. It was a lesson Amos did not fail to recognize over his relatively short but highly eventful life.

He was born in the back seat of a Redneck bus rolling down highway Kingdom Come. His brother, being just two-and-a-half years old, was distracted at the time trying to steal a cookie from his mother's purse.

The newborn shot out into the world into the arms of his father in the blink of an eye, not like the long and torturous birth of her first child, Abrekapocus. That one, who they came to nickname Abe, had played the drama queen from the get-go, making his mother endure two false labors and twenty-seven hours of pushing and shoving. His father, Theo Dopolis, had a mind to call him Beelzebubba, but by the time all the moaning and groaning was over, he was passed out, too drunk to be involved in the official naming of the little beast.

This new birth couldn't have been more different, and so too was the child. The labor, if you could call it that, could easily have been recorded in the Guinness Book of World Records as the shortest ever. For YoYo Mama, his mother, an artistic woman and brilliant cellist, it was an unexpected relief. Her water broke and presto-changeo, there he was, with not a mark or blotch on him. His tongue looked a little off kilter, though, seemingly sucking incessantly on the roof of his mouth. And YoYo found out soon enough that the breastfeeding routine had no hope in hell of working out.

The first image that caught his mother's eye after he popped out into the world was a sign for the town they were passing through, Amos, not far outside of Shatnopoopoo, in the Great Territory of Tango Sea (aptly named for the expertise of its water dancers). 'A wonderful name for my child,' she thought. Amos, that is. And, being a deeply religious woman, thought Moses would complement it perfectly as his second name. 'Yes,' she thought, 'I'll name him after a man of the cloth and call him Amos Moses.'

Theo didn't have much to say about the naming of his second son, either. After he had grappled onto the slippery little wiggler when he was born, Theo had immediately fainted. When he came to twenty minutes later and found out the boy's name, he mulled it over. He thought it either odd or ironic (he wasn't sure which) that he had two sons who had first initials that combined to form AA, something that gave him the heebie-jeebies. As he began to tremble and sweat, the thought of it made him think about his life-long friend Jack, who never failed to set him at ease. Yes, Jack Daniels is who he needed to talk to. But at the moment it was impossible, being stuck on the bus with an empty flask.

He looked over at the infant and it made him shiver. 'The skinny little wiggler,' he thought, 'has the most curious eyes.' He nudged YoYo, 'Hey baby, with those eyes of his drifting around in all directions, he's gonna get his share of humiliatin growin up.'

She sneered at him, 'Give him a break, you louse. He's just taking in everything around him. And that's a whole lot more than most people do in life.'

He thought about it for a minute and said to himself, 'Mayhaps she's right. And I could make use of someone like that in due time.' Theo studied the infant closely over the next several hours as the boy spluttered and fidgeted about. It wasn't easy though, with that piercing stare he would get from Amos, that is to say when his sky-blue eyes weren't googling around in all directions. He had the oddest ring of slightly curly blond hair encircling the top of his head. With not another sprig of hair to be seen anywhere else, it looked something like the decorative icing around the top edge of a birthday cake.

When they locked eyes, Theo felt the hairs on the back of his neck rise and thought, 'There's sumpin funny about ye, boy. Cain't quite put me finger on it but fer some reason I think I might get some pretty good mileage outta ye somewhere down the line.'

Looking at Abe, who was stuffing his mouth with cookies, and then at Amos, it made him wonder, 'How can two children from the same parents be so differnt?' There was the first-born, tough and meaty at birth, a full nine-pounds eight-ounces with everything dark, skin, eyes, and hair. And now this one, barely six pounds of sinew and bones, as skinny and long as a beanpole with the tiniest hands you'd ever see, and a complexion so fair he almost appeared to be opaque.

'Next stop,' the bus driver bellowed out over the PA system, 'Bacon County Line in the Great Territory of Gorgeous!'

When the bus pulled into the station, Theo rose from his seat and whispered to YoYo, 'Just goin out to get some Doritos and Red Bull, baby. Be right back.'

'Get some diapers, too,' she said.

He leaned over with that ridiculous grin he'd display whenever he thought he was about to say something funny, 'Don't think they got any small enough for a skinny tadpole like him,' and he laughed.

YoYo was incensed. 'Just hurry in there before the bus leaves. And stay away from the liquor section,' she hissed.

He made his way down the aisle and when he stepped off the bus, he scrunched his face up and said under his breath, 'How kin sumpin that smells so good when it's cooked come from sumpin that smells so friggin bad when it ain't?'

He hustled over to the 7-Eleven to pick up his refreshments of Doritos and whiskey. When he left the store, he crouched down and snuck around the back to have a good long pull on the bottle. As he was refilling his flask a wino approached him and asked for a cigarette. Theo obliged and after having a smoke and a couple of drinks, he noticed the bus leaving the station.

Knowing he would never catch up to it, he shrugged his shoulders and said to his new friend, 'There goes me two little boys, mister. I sure don't mind losin their mammy, but those boys coulda been some good use to me when they got themselves growed-up. That older one is as shifty as they come, shifty as an opossum, I'd say. And the newborn, well, God only knows what's comin up fer him.'

The wino noticed the trace of a tear in the corner of Theo's eye.

He patted him on the shoulder and said, 'I feel for ya, brother. Now, can I have another haul offa that thar bottle?'

***

When the bus started up to leave, YoYo craned her neck over toward the store. Theo was nowhere to be seen and she desperately needed the diapers. As much as she hated to admit it, she needed him, too. He was the one who controlled the money, and all she had on her was the measly twenty dollars that he allotted her every week.

The bus pulled away from the station and YoYo hung her head and began to cry. 'Why,' she thought, 'did I ever get involved with that buffoon? Boozer, adulterer, gambler. How, *how* in the world did I ever end up with him?' And then she thought again, 'Oh, right. That con he played did it to me. The one where he convinced me he was the agent and primary financial supporter of the Electrifying Luminescent Orchestration. Yeah, and there I was thinking about a classical music gig *at last*, maybe long-term, instead of doing those back-alley sideshows surrounded by freaks and pimps.' She never had a problem with their music, ELO that is, thought it was great in fact. The problem was Theo. He was connected to them financially to be sure, owned copies of every album they ever produced, but that was about as far as it went. And when it came to him being their "Agent", yeah, right. He owned a two-bit used records store where the only records in his inventory seemed to be scratched ELO albums with defaced covers. But he did have money, somehow. And it just walked out the door, leaving her high and dry. Life was tough enough as it was, she thought, and feared it was about to get tougher.

She sighed as she stroked Amos' head and said to him, 'Finding food and shelter might not be easy, little angel.'

She continued her journey south, and now that Theo wasn't along with her in his search for still more ELO records, she hoped she would find a place of support and refuge. As luck would have it, she realized that the LMT Club was just two towns away. The club had its own radio station and TV show, which she regularly tuned into, and it was obvious they had lots of love, too. 'After all,' she thought, 'that was their calling card, wasn't it? Right there in their title, the Love Me Tender Club. How could they turn their backs on me?' She desperately needed food, shelter, and nurturing for her newborn son and his growing elder brother.

As the bus pulled into the station at Camp Granada, Gorgeous, she disembarked with her one suitcase, two kids, and cello case in tow. She immediately headed for the lone telephone outside the station mounted on the wall alongside what turned out to be some very helpful graffiti: JIMBO ROCKS - call the LMT Club 1-999-999-9999, and TAMBO ROLLS - call the LMT Club 1-999-999-9999, or find us on Twitter @Jimbo&TamboLove-Makers. YoYo knew they were a modern group of worshippers and had seen their act plenty of times, guitars, drums, horns and a string section. It sounded heavenly. 'And perhaps,' she thought hopefully, 'there would be a spot for a cellist.'

She made the call, hoping against hope they would take her in. On the third ring a high-pitched woman's voice with a southern drawl answered, 'How y'all dooooin?'

'Oh, hello. This is YoYo Mama calling. I'm so sorry to bother you, but...' and she began to cry. Between sobs she spluttered out, 'I'm in so much trouble and desperately need some help.'

'Well this is Tambo, honey-chile, and you sure as the sky is blue called the ko-rrect place fer that. Just what is it you need, sugar?'

'Oh, thank you, thank you, Mrs. Tambo. I watch you all the

time on TV and love your show.'

'That's so kindly of you to say, sweetie-pie. Where are y'all callin from, honey-buns?'

'I'm at the bus station in Camp Granada with my two babies. One was just born outside of Amos in Tango Sea and my husband abandoned us when the bus stopped in Bacon County.'

'Oh, heaven's above dear chile, that is a scandalous turn of events! Someone actually getting off the bus in that horrid smellin place, I mean. What xactly kin I do fer ya, baby-girl?'

'I need a place to stay where I can take care of my children for a while until I can get my life sorted out, Mrs. Tambo.'

'Well, this is your lucky day, believe it or don't, take your pick. That's the business we're in over here at the Love Me Tender Club, lovin and a helpin folks who's in trouble. I'll send a car over to get you this very instant and we'll have y'all prayin and a singin and a dancin quicker than you kin say "Granny get yer gun".'

'Oh, thank you so much, Mrs. Tambo, but what we really need now is something to eat.'

'O course, o course, little ducky. But let's get one thing straight right off. Tambo's me name and lovin's me game. The title Missus just don't work with that. You hearin me right, chile?'

'Oh yes, Tambo. Thank you so much again, Tambo.'

Tambo smiled and said, 'Now I'm hearin ya proper, darlin. I'll send a car to pick you up pronto and see you soon. Tweedilee-Do!'

YoYo was in tears when she began to thank Tambo again, but the line had already gone dead.

Jimbo entered the room and gave Tambo a squeeze from behind just as she ended the call. 'What's the latest, lamb-chops?' he asked.

'Oh, I is absotively over the moon, Jimbo. A young waylaid waif is on her way over. She just had a baby, praise the Lord above in heaven, and she needs a place to stay. Kin you tell Jethro to go pick her up at the bus station in Camp Granada? Her name is YoYo Mama.'

'Sure as shootin, pumpkin. I'll go get him now. I think he's out at the ceement pond.'

Jimbo tracked Jethro down and told him to go pick up YoYo. He threw Jethro the keys to the SUV and added, 'She's got a newborn with her, so be careful with the little tadpole.'

Jethro smiled from ear to ear, happy to be going out for a drive and said, 'Oh, I will, giant Jimbo.'

When he got in the car, he rolled the windows down and sped away. He turned on the radio and thought it was a funny thing, after what Jimbo had called the newborn, that his favorite song by Silly Elfin was playing, and he began to sing along.

♫ He's a toad, my friend

He ain't no saint, he's just a toad, my friend

In spite of that he'll seem cherubic now and again

But he's a toad, I tell ya it's true my friend ♫

Happily cruising along in his favorite automobile, he smelled it long before he rounded the bend. As he came around the turn, sure enough there it was, a dead skunk in the middle of his lane and it was stinking to high heaven. In a moment of panic trying to avoid the dead critter, he swerved to his left. Fortunately, there was no oncoming traffic, but unfortunately it propelled him onto a collision course with the animal's stink sac. A direct hit, in fact, which had a most unpleasant effect.

His eyes began to water, and his nose became a spout of, well, you know. Luckily the bus station was just around the next corner. When he pulled in, he inadvertently jumped the curb, due to his impaired vision, and clipped a fire hydrant, bringing the car to a stop right outside the front door.

Sitting inside watching the events unfold outside, YoYo wondered how many drinks *that* guy had in him. Water was shooting up out of the fire hydrant when Jethro emerged from the car, and he became drenched by the towering fountain of water. He scratched his head of thick jet-black hair and YoYo thought she heard him exclaim, 'Who in tarnation put that thing there?'

He entered the bus station and looked back and forth from left to right, searching for a woman with two young children. Not seeing her, he bellowed out, 'Anyone herebouts by the name of YoYo?'

Her heart sank, but she tentatively raised her hand and said, 'That's my name, sir.'

'I'll be danged,' he said, 'there ya wuz right in the front of me all along. I'm Jethro, and Jimbo sent me here to save ya. Come on, girl. Let's get them little rascals into the car and skedaddle outta here afore the po-leece come.'

They scrambled outside and when they got in the car they heard the sirens wailing. Jethro's shoulders slumped when he looked in the rearview mirror and saw two police cars and a fire engine pulling into the station. The lead firefighter approached Jethro's car and noted to one of the officers, 'I don't see a fire, but I see rain.'

The officer smiled and said, 'That's a good thing. Let's see what this bonehead is up to.'

He looked in the car and noticed the children and baggage in the back seat. He turned toward the soaking wet handsome young man, and what looked to be his wife, in the front and asked, 'What's going on here? You have some ID you can provide to me, young man, license and registration.'

The firefighter left to shut off the main water valve while Jethro produced the documents.

The officer perused the documents and asked Jethro, 'You authorized to operate this vee-hicle, sonny? I see it's registered to Jimbo Banker.'

'Yes siree, yer honor. I be workin fer him and he done told me to pick up this destitute gal an bring her on down to his abodiodoh.'

'Abodiodoh?'

'Yepper, abodiodoh be what he calls his own place.'

'Craziest thing I ever heard, abodiodoh. Any which way, youngin, Jimbo and Tambo run that charity called the LMT Club, don't they?'

'They sho nough do, offreecer. They's gonna help this girl who done got stranded somehow or t'other.'

'Well, sonny, in that case we'll just let you off with a warning today. Oh, and Jethro, by-the-way, no personal offence intended, but you otta get yourself cleaned up, you stink worse than a wet dog in a fart factory.'

'Yes sir, constabular. I hit a skunk, so as soon as I get to the tomato juice store I'll be getting right in the tub.'

The officer handed back the documents and Jethro drove off the curb and down the road while YoYo stuffed her nose with tissue paper. He looked over at her and said, 'I got some splainin to do bout the dent in the bumper and all the stink when we git back. Mayhaps ye kin distract Jimbo till I come up with some story to feed him.'

'Why not just tell him you had an accident trying to avoid a skunk? That way you kill two birds with one stone.'

He had to think about that for a minute. Having to consider the accident, the skunk, two birds, and a stone threw too many balls in the air for him to contemplate at one time.

When he finally got it, he burst out, 'Golllly girl! Ain't you just the cleverest thing God put on this great green earth!'

She hung her head and wondered what in the world she was getting herself and the boys into.

As Jethro entered the driveway Tambo rushed, or at least waddled hurriedly, out of the house. She engulfed YoYo in a bear hug when she got out of the gleaming black SUV and YoYo thought she heard something snap in her back.

Eager to greet her, Jimbo was right behind Tambo, all a-smiling. YoYo noted that familiar gleam in his eyes. That "Praise the Lord" look he often displayed when he was leading his orchestra in heavenly worship on TV. She wasn't all too sure now if her assessment of his facial expression had been correct, as it appeared somewhat sinister now that she saw him in real life. He pushed Tambo aside and when YoYo extended her hand in greeting, he gave it a wet sloppy kiss. He bowed slightly and then boastfully introduced himself as Jimbo, faithful servant and obedient proclaimer of the Lord above in heaven.

Not to be upstaged, Tambo pushed Jimbo back as he wiped the spittle off his mouth. 'Welcome to our lovin home, sweet-pea,' she said. 'Y'all must be sooo tarred after the tempest and turmoil that's befallen ya. Whew, I kin tell ye ain't had a proper warshin up in days, chile. Mayhaps weeks even!'

'Oh, thank you both so much for taking us in. I swear I'll try to get myself together and out of your hair as soon as I can,' YoYo assured her.

'Don't you worry your pretty little head bout that, snookums. But I'm a curious one, what in tarnation is in the case you got there?' Tambo asked.

'That's my sole source of income sitting there, my cello. Not that I can put it to much use now, what with the two boys hanging off me.'

'A cello?' Jimbo beamed. 'May perchance we have a place fer you. I always forever dreamt of having a cellist,' and he blushed, 'in our orchestra, I mean.'

An awkward pause ensued as Tambo took note of the sparkle

in his eye, as did YoYo. Tambo broke the silence, 'Let's get y'all fed and warshed up, queeny. We have plenty o room fer y'all to bed down in later. Cummon inside and I'll get Ellie-Mae to prepare a big mess of crawdads with polk salad and collard greens.'

'Now yer talkin my lingo, cream-cakes,' Jimbo piped in. 'I'm so hungry I could eat a gator.'

The boys were sleeping in the back seat of the SUV and Jimbo bellowed to Jethro and Ellie-Mae to carry them into the house. He went over to the vehicle with them and recoiled, twisting and turning about at the stench. He managed to get his coughing and gagging under control enough to say, 'What in the land o glory did you get yerself into, Jethro? That stinks worser than a dead skunk!'

'That's xactly what it wuz, big Jimbo. I is so sorry. I clipped a cedar tree tryin to avoid the critter but hit him all the same.'

'Lordy, Jethro,' Jimbo said when he saw the red paint on the damaged fender, 'you thinkin I just fell offa the pumpkin truck? Ain't no red cedars round hereabouts, they're all over in the next county.'

'Oh, no, Jimbo-bubba. That thar be from the fire hy..., um, I mean, yeah, yeah, that's xactly what it wuz, a red cedar, it wuz,' Jethro beamed, thinking he had been clever enough to cover his tracks, so to speak.

Jimbo eyed him suspiciously, rubbed his fleshy chin, and said, 'Hmm, I never did see a red cedar round these parts afore, and even iffin there wuz, that thar scrape be lookin like paint to me. Never no mind fer now though, we gotta git this young lady and her youngins sorted out. Mayhaps I best be getting ya to drive the hog-tied Lincoln until we get this here damage fixed up.'

Jethro broke out into a broad smile, 'Gollly, Uncle Jimbo, I love drivin that hot rod. Gives me plenty o room to stretch out me long legs.'

'Yes, I be knowin that's true. Yer a tall drink o water, alright. But I be warnin ya this, don't ye be racin any o those long white cadillacs I seen crusin round these parts lately or ye'll be pushin up daisies out in the back forty, lickety-split.'

Jethro grinned sheepishly and kicked at the dirt, 'Daisy? Oh, no siree, don't worry bout that, Jimbo. I usually push her up when I get her out in the barn over yonder.'

Jimbo shook his head, wondering why in the blazes he ever took the poor lad in. Then he thought back to Jethro's story. A big handsome guy who failed to make a go of it building dams, of all things, in Beaverly Hills. Found him on the side of the road over in the Great Territory of Ark-I-Saw drinking Apple Pie Moonshine and figured he'd play well to the TV audiences. And that he did. They loved his naiveté and valiant, but failed attempts at inventiveness in the silly biblical skits he performed in. Yes, the poor boy had increased the ratings, no doubt about it.

'Oh well,' Jimbo thought, 'he be a pile o trouble with the vee-hicles, but leastwise he ain't into the evil kinda stuff I been seein goin on round herebouts lately.'

Meanwhile, Tambo had led YoYo into the house and when they entered, YoYo stopped and stood in wonder. 'What is this place?' she thought. The house from the outside was rather unassuming, a modern two-story of no great distinction whatsoever. But inside it was stunning, solid hardwood flooring in a coloring she'd only heard about, seemingly a whiter shade of pale. The matching staircase, banister, and door and window trim completed the effect of being in heaven.

Jethro and Ellie-Mae came in and deposited the boys on the luxurious sofa. YoYo was fearful as she approached Tambo and said, 'Little Amos is due for a feeding and I'm afraid it could get messy.'

Tambo surveyed the little baby and exclaimed, 'Well lordy lord above, ain't he the most heavenly and righteous lookin creature what *ever* was born! And I'll be danged, lookit that halo runnin round the top of his head. Mother Mary!'

YoYo blushed, 'That's his hair, but I sure like the way you put it, Tambo.'

Tambo smiled, 'You get that angel all fed up and have not a care in this whole wide world bout nuttin, sugar-cakes. I'll get y'all a towel and tell Ellie-Mae to set up the baby crib in one of the guest rooms fer later.' She left the room to get Ellie-Mae, all in a dither with the recent turn of events.

As she was waiting for Tambo to return, YoYo sat in amazement at the tasteful and expensive furnishings and artwork. She wondered how they could afford it, given the cheesy show they produced.

When Jimbo entered the room he gave her the small nursing blanket Tambo had given him. He sat down beside YoYo and gazed at the infant and seemingly fell into a trance from the aura emanating from him. She draped the blanket over her shoulder and said, just as Tambo returned, 'Thanks for the blanket, but I'm not sure it will be big enough.'

'Oh, peachykins, don't y'all fret about nothin,' Tambo said. 'We'll have Ellie-Mae fix up anythin that makes a mess round here.' Jimbo snapped out of his trance and was waiting in anticipation for the show to begin when Tambo grabbed his wrist, 'Cummon, Jimbo, let's go out poolside and you kin ogle me as I put on another layer of make-up.' Jimbo's face sagged, as he was curious to view Amos' meal offering, but he rose from the chair and, attempting to mask his condition, followed Tambo, stiff-legged, out to the pool.

After the messy feeding, YoYo put the boys to bed in the guest room Ellie-Mae had set up, and then had a fine meal with her hosts. She turned in early and as she lay her head down to sleep, she kept turning over in her mind a little rhythm she liked, ♫ Tambo saved, Tambo saved, Tambo saved my life tonight ♫.

The next morning, they all had breakfast together and Jimbo asked her what kind of music she played.

'I have a sequent chord,' she whispered.

'Oh? Do tell, sweet YoYo. How does it go, and would it be a pleasure to our Adored?' Jimbo asked.

'It's kind of a funny tune, it has a horse and a hitch, and then there's a finer stall with a chamber rift.'

Jimbo looked baffled, 'Well, tie me to a Christian chair and give me a haircut! That is *very* unusual, YoYo.'

They began talking about the different types of music they

loved. They found they shared an interest not only in gospel music, but also country and western and country rock. Tambo suggested they try out a few tunes *a cappella*, and, as if they were struck by divine intervention from the great Johnny Smash himself and his talented wife Moon Farter, Jimbo began singing bass, with Tambo singing tenor, and little YoYo piping right in.

> ♫ No more cereal, I got a notion
> My oh my, Adored, my oh my
> We'll be on the throne, I'm just sayin
> With a pie, Adored, with a pie ♫

> ♫ Tambo stuffed her face (Jimbo stuffed with her)
> YoYo and bitty brothers conjoined the din
> We is high, Adored, high on pie ♫

They had a fine time carrying on from there, exploring all kinds of gospel music, eating every pie in sight, fresh and frozen alike, with not a drop of ice cream to be found in the aftermath. When the mayhem carried them into Weird Al's food tunes, YoYo knew she was in. 'Finally,' she thought, 'I have a place to call home where I can safely raise Amos and Abe. And play my cello in a real band!'

Acting every bit the sideshow barker, Jimbo bellowed to the jostling crowd outside the Hootenanay House, 'Step right up, step right up! Get yer tickets afore we sell em all out, folks!' He knew who they were coming to see, the one who packed them in every Sunday morning. None other than YoYo. She had become so popular that he had to turn them away at the gates. Ever since she joined the Oak Ridge Gospel Yodelers, the place had been bursting at the seams for every event.

He was bursting at the seams, too, in more ways than one. The number of people tuning into the TV and radio shows jumped five-fold, which increased the price of advertising and the amount of revenue rolling into the coffers. Gate receipts and concession sales at the monthly "Bible Bustin" shows they started up were through the roof. And the merch booth was hard to keep stocked, with everyone wanting to latch onto a piece of memorabilia. Record sales skyrocketed and Jimbo was hard-pressed to churn out new vinyl fast enough to cash in on the phenomenon.

But they weren't the only seams that were bursting, or things Jimbo was hard-pressed about. So were the seams of his pants. Try as he did to satisfy his lust for YoYo, Tambo just kept too close an eye on him. And the girl, she knew what he was up to, and knew how to slip his grasp and his slobbering hand-kisses. No matter how much he played the gentleman, which had never failed to work before, she refused to be taken in. Well, in that way anyhow.

Apart from Jimbo's unwelcome advances, YoYo appreciated the shelter she was offered. And they never insisted she find her own place. She was ecstatic that Amos got to play the role of baby Jesus in the Christmas nativity skit, and Tambo was happy to have the two boys to pamper and shower gifts upon. They were a handful though, no doubt about it. She could see from the get-go that Abe was a controller. Maybe not so unusual for a first born, she thought. But what did she know, having no practical experience, being *barren* and all. And poor Amos. The child was an awkward one physically, but he took everything Abe threw at him in good humor. And he also took everything in around him, most of all Abe's mistakes. His favorite pastime was listening to music and was down-right transfixed when the trumpet solos began, clapping his hands and tapping his feet in an enthusiastic, if somewhat off-beat, rhythm.

But Jimbo was torn between Tambo's newfound sense of purpose and the money that was rolling in, and the mayhem the boys brought to the household and the money that was rolling out to support theM.

Following a late afternoon session with his accounting firm, he knew he had to speak to Tambo about a troubling and delicate topic. He had a strategy when it came to things like that - slather on the butter and hope it sticks.

He approached her cautiously and said, 'We need to talk, sweetie-pussims.'

'Oh, what's all a troublin yo hurtin head, stud-muffin?'

'Well, buttercup, the accountants are frettin over your expenditures on make-up, like eyeliner, lipstick, hairspray, blush, application brushes, those kinda things. They said it looks like you must be getting the mascara shipped in by truck, sugar-doll, and sumpin about a portable magnifying glass.'

'I *know* what comes in a make-up kit, big diddy-daddy, and you know I need every single one of those creams, sticks, gels, sprays, lotions, and applicators to look my most appealin to y'all, and fer the show, too, Jimbo-bo. There are so many products these days to make a gal feel special. No wonder we had to build that little-ole make-up Sugar Shack out by the pool fer me to work my magic every mornin. And that magnifying glass, the one they just deelibered the other day, mounted on the stand the way it is, that is the most precious piece of ingenuosness I ever did see, honey-cakes. It will let me inspect every little flaw, er, I mean, imperfection I need to cover up. I think ya might need to adjust it a bit fer me height though, Jimbo. I cain't seem to use it the way it's set up.'

'Aw, honeybunches, I know you're a doll-face one way or t'other. But that's bout as useful as an inflatable dartboard. What you need is a magnifying *mirror*, peachy-pear.'

'Shucks, I knew there wuz sumpin bout it that wasn't right. I'll send it back tomorra and get the ko-rrect one deelibered.'

'How bout we do this fer that heap o other stuff, sugar-shuggy, maybe we kin bulk order and get some discount pricin. That should keep the bean-counters at bay. What do you think?'

'I think ye is a stupendulous hubby-bubbs. I'll arrange that and y'all won't have to natter yer noggin about it agin.'

'Yer a knock-out, honey-pie. By the way, where is YoYo?'

Tambo shot him a suspicious look. 'Don't ya remember? She's out with the band celebratin Lay-Low's birthday. Why, what's up, sneaky, er, make that snooky-snooks.'

'Jus wonderin, li'l nutter-girl. Let's go have dinner now, I'm absatibly famishin.'

The two boys were out at a sleepover, so they had a quiet dinner together, which was a relief in one way. It was a blessing there was no crying or food flying, but it made for some dodgy moments, Jimbo thinking about YoYo out on the town, and Tambo thinking about Jimbo thinking about YoYo out on the town.

Jimbo tried to ease the tension, 'Sugar-plum, we needs to be findin a way to get that sweet girl singing in the band. I'm sure she kin sing whilst she's strokin that bow.'

'Oh, Jimbo, you's always been sooo enthralled bout strokin this and a strokin that, but I'll tell ya this, and it's a true fact. She'd be a right fine singer in the band, there's no doubtin about it, but that's all she gonna be good fer, iffin ye git me drift, jigglin Jimbo.'

A sheepish grin appeared on Jimbo's face, 'It only happened that one time, blessed-baby. Now it's just me eyes what wander, lovey-lumps, ye knows that. Ain't nothin else bout me wanders hither and thither.' He could tell she needed a little cooling down and wanted to give her some of his love. He wasn't fooling when he started to sing one of her favorite songs by Zed Schleppin.

♫ I'z just drooooooling
When our Lord is sooooothing
He'll surely give us
Some of his refuuuuueling ♫

♫ That day when ya cried
After I had lied and lied
It came down from above
It came down from above ♫

♫ He gave me you as a dove, wooooooow
Now I know yer my drug, wooooooow
He gave me you as a dove, wooooooow
You fit me like a glove ♫

Tambo smiled and gave him a wink. 'You a good man, Jimbo, and I knows it, but just don't let me see ya lurkin roundbout her room late at night getting all higgledy-piggledy like, or ye'll be regrettin all bout it the next mornin-time.'

'Yer gittin me all hot and bothered, teasin-Tambo. Let's turn in fer the night and have some rollie-pollie time.'

'Oh, heavens to Betsy, Jimbo, you is a real rascal tonight.'

'Yes, tis true. I'm picturing us climbin our stairway to heavenly love right at this very moment.'

Tambo smiled and winked again. 'Then grab that banana cream pie and can o whipped cream, slippery-son, and foller me. I done got a little surprise fer ya tonight.'

He became overly excited thinking about going to bed with his sweet Queen and started singing as he pulled up the rear, and pushed it, too (her bottom, that is) as Tambo always had a difficult time getting her large bottom up the staircase.

♫ Aww, I want her to bake that pie just right
Aww, I want to eat it deep through the night
Aww, I'll surely cram it in my mouth
That awesome pearl knows I'll come knocking
when it's all browned ♫

22

It's a good thing the boys had made some friends, well, one at least. The poor little boy and his parents didn't know what they were in for when they took Abe and Amos in for a sleepover that night. But it made no-never-mind to YoYo, she was going to go out and have some fun for a change.

The club wasn't too far away, Darlyn's Rockin Roadhouse and Brontosaurus-on-a-Stick Shack, so she walked over just before sunset. Darlyn always invited the best rock, blues, and disco acts from around the country, both old and new, to play at his venue. Real players like Skinny Leonard, Wanderin Stevie, Casey & the Moonshine Band, Boss Rags, and believe it or not, even the latest phenom, the avant-garde Baby HaHa. YoYo thought she was awesome, and especially loved her latest hit, "Born This Way", and not many people would disagree with her.

Having had the kids early in life, YoYo never had time to be a club girl, so she wasn't used to the shenanigans that could go on in a place like Darlyn's. When the music fired up and the dancing began, it was more than she could ask for.

Darlyn knew talent when he saw it and knew all about YoYo's phenomenal rise on the local scene. Intrigued by how a cello might compliment his band in his jam sessions, he approached her and offered his hand, 'Let's do a little Karaoke duet, sweet girl.'

She was gob smacked, the great Darlyn wanting to check out her pipes, and maybe, just maybe, something else too. Which wouldn't be the worst thing in the world, she thought, when she looked at the sad lot around her, not to mention how goll-darn handsome he was.

'Tell me something about yourself and I'll do a little improv with some lyrics,' he said.

She blurted out the first thing that popped into her head, 'I have a little boy named Amos.'

She rose from her chair and, hand in hand, they approached the stage. He whispered to her, 'I'm sick and tired of singing my own songs, so I'll ad lib some lyrics about Amos to the melody of a song I like by Sob Bigger.'

YoYo asked, 'What song is it?'

He tried to ease her anxiety, 'Don't worry, just follow my lead. It's called "Kathmandu".'

'Oh, good,' she said, 'I know that one.'

YoYo was a bit nervous when they climbed up on the stage, and she told Darlyn she hadn't sung publicly for a long time. He gave her a wink and a pat on her bum. 'I'll sing the verses and you just join in on the chorus.' She responded with a smile and the music began.

> ♫ I'm not sure what that Cat can do
> We'll see in the end if he smells like poo
> He might give us all a real big scare
> And it could make ya bluuuue
> C-c-c-c-c-c Cat-can-do
> He's the guy who might even try a coup
> When he grows he might give us a scare
> Oh, what that Cat can dooooo ♫

YoYo had a quizzical look on her face from the lyrics he was singing. Darlyn gave her a little nudge and a smile, and whispered, 'Don't ask me where that came from. Let's do the chorus,' and YoYo stumbled through it.

> ♫ C-c-c-c-c-c Cat-can-do
> His game will be about throwin dog-doo
> He'll be a man without the faintest clue
> C-c-c-c-c-c Cat-can-do
> C-c-c-c-c-c Cat-can-do ♫

> ♫ He's just a hick to the least and most
> When they see him eating grits on toast
> He'll be a pesky ass, sumpin like rump roast
> He'll surely make them bluuuue

And then spew on about all those he hates
Most times he'll seem unhinged and quite irate
Then he'll be runnin with his name on the slate
Ya never know what he might dooooo ♫

The crowd was in stitches as the lyrics became more and more bizarre, and they joined in as best they could at the end.

♫ When he teams up with all his peers
Ye'll hear nothin but taunts and jeers
And then ye'll realize all yer fears
When ya see what that Cat-can-do
C-c-c-c-c Cat-can-do
Yes he will surely surely make ya blue
Oh, what that Cat will dooooo! ♫

The audience was jumping and bopping around and gave them a rousing ovation when they finished the song.

As YoYo turned to leave the stage she whispered to him, 'You might be a hunk, Darlyn, but how could you sing about my little boy Amos like that?'

He grabbed her and gave her a kiss full on the lips and said, 'No offence intended, sweet YoYo, but that's the kind of thing that happens when you're jamming. You never know what's going to come out.'

He escorted her to her table and gave her his phone number, telling her he had a gig across town he had to get to. She sat down, dumbfounded, and watched him as he walked out the door.

Her friends gave her a mighty cheer and ordered drinks all around in celebration. However, YoYo didn't realize the power of a shooter when they began ordering them up in rounds. After three Gin tonics and four shooters she was over the moon, flying high as a kite and having the time of her life.

What hit her next was quite unexpected. With the disco ball rotating clockwise, it was like her brain began to spin in the opposite direction, which made for an unusual sensation in her stomach. A sensation she remembered from her early days of pregnancy. Little did she know that one of her fellow bandmates had spiked her last drink with ecstasy, hoping for some action later. She'd already had to slap him a couple of times to keep his hands off her.

Much to his chagrin, YoYo rose from the table on the pretext of going to the restroom and then snuck out of the club and headed for home. The relatively short walk should have taken twenty minutes but given her condition she was a full hour and a half getting there. Being so late, and knowing the kids were out for the night, she didn't want to wake up Jimbo and Tambo, so she decided to sit out near the pool in Tambo's luxurious make-up chair.

***

Now, Jimbo and Tambo never were early risers, except for Sunday mornings so they could make it to their radio show on time. Unfortunately, this wasn't Sunday morning. Tambo rolled over in the waterbed, which almost catapulted Jimbo onto the floor on the other side. 'Whoa, lambkins, easy does it. I'm gonna break my neck one of these days when you do that,' he said.

'Aww, shucks, Jimmy-Jimbo, I is so sorry. What time is it anyhow, we should probly get this glorious day goin.'

Jimbo groaned, 'Oh, sweet child, it's eleven o'clock. Let's rest a little more.'

Tambo nudged him, 'Well, daddy-cakes, we kin stay for a piece more as long as you want to rock the boat a little bit, if you get my drift.'

When they came out of the bedroom at twelve o'clock they had a blissful brunch, a stack of flapjacks slathered in maple syrup, 8 rashers of bacon each, and fresh squeezed orange juice. After they both showered up, not together (as that would have exceeded the maximum capacity of the space, given their collective girth), they emerged again from the bedroom; Tambo ready to begin the two-hour reconstruction job from the neck up. She grabbed a cup of coffee to make her way out into the blazing sun to her Sugar Shack and hollered back to Jimbo, 'Why don't y'all find out where those two little bugger boys are, sweet-doll-o-mine! They should be back from the sleepover by now.' As she approached the pool, she noticed a foul smell.

As he was dialing, Jimbo heard an ungodly scream. 'Jimmy, Jimmy Jimbo. Jimmy Jimbo-Bo-Bo. Call the far department, call the far department!'

He peered out the kitchen window and yelled back, 'What in God's great heaven is goin on, sweet-candy?'

'Sumpin's wrong with YoYo,' she wailed. 'Her hair is half burnt off her. Oh, my lord! Oh, my sweet Lord up above us all! Hurry Jimbo! Cummeeeer, pronto!'

He rushed out to the pool to find YoYo slumped over in Tambo's exquisite make-up chair, directly under the magnifying glass, and said, 'Oh dear. Oh, dear me. Is she breathing, cream-puffy-puff?'

'I haven't the faintest idear, Rollie-Pollie Papa. I cain't get near her cause she stinks so bad.'

He pushed Tambo aside and said, 'Let me check, jelly-bean.'

He discovered YoYo had no pulse and decided to try to revive her. His problem was that the only thing he knew about CPR was that two sets of lips were supposed to come together, and the rest was a mystery. He decided to enjoy the moment, but then recoiled from the foul smell. 'I'll call the mergency responders, bubble-gum. Hand me the phone, will ya,' he said to Tambo.

When the paramedics arrived and attended to YoYo, the first one looked at Jimbo and said, 'Appears she's ridin the elevator to the Almighty as we speak, Mister.'

Tambo was horrified. 'Y'all mean she be dead? Ain't nuttin y'all kin do fer the poor waif?'

'She's dead alright, deader than disco, I'd say, Missus. Looks like a case of Cerebellum Hyperthermia, judging by the power o that magnifying glass, not to mention the little bitty hole in her head. See what I mean, right there.' He pointed to a spot on the crown of YoYo's head.

Jimbo and Tambo shrank back in horror. 'Well butter my butt and call me a biscuit,' Jimbo exclaimed, 'ain't that the most scurrilous thing on God's green earth.'

'Well, that may or mayn't be, Mister,' the second paramedic said, 'but one way or t'other, we gotta haul her off to the meat freezer and let the aww-topsiologist do his thang with her. Oh, oh, several pardons Missus, y'all know what I was tryin to say, right?'

Tambo eyed him sideways, and Jimbo spoke up, 'Listen here, sonny-bubba, there ain't gonna be no kinda hanky-panky goin on with this lovely little cadaver, er, cellist. This is gonna put the ruins to our fortunate turn in life and we won't have any scandalous happenins heaped on top o the pile o mess we is already gonna have with this unfortunate *accident*.'

The paramedic tried to reassure him. 'No sir, no siree. There won't be a hair out of place on that sweet chile's head, I can assure you that's a fact. Well, other than what's already missin.'

Jimbo gave him a scornful look. 'Ye's bout as funny as chocolate ice cream on possum pie, young feller. Oh, dang, wrong expression. Tambo happens to think that's a most heavenly combination. Irregardlessness, git the poor gal on outta here, nice and secret-like. Ya hearin me right?'

'Yes sir, yes sir. We'll just get to work and haul her on outta here, lickety-split.'

The paramedics proceeded to bag YoYo up and place her on the stretcher. As they began to wheel her out through the house to the ambulance, the doorbell rang. Tambo was fit to be tied, not wanting there to be any public scandal. She waved the paramedics aside to hide in the parlor and tentatively opened the door, to be confronted by two happy and two angry faces.

The boys burst into the room and promptly bolted for the pool, while their now former friend's parents scowled and simply growled, 'Here's their stuff,' dumping everything on the doorstep. They both spun around and stomped down the walkway.

Relieved that the boys were back, Tambo waved goodbye and

called out, 'Thank y'all, lookin forward to doin it all agin soon, ya hear?'

The parents, without looking back, delivered a unified response, each giving her the two-fisted finger.

Chapter 7 – You Gotta Know When To Hold Em, And When To Fold Em

No, Jimbo couldn't abide it, two young boys running wild hither and thither. All the precious furnishings they worked so hard to acquire getting trashed due to the throwing of balls, the wrestling, and the stumbling about. 'What's with that child Amos, lollypop? Three years old and a true child of God but cain't keep hisself upright no better than a fish kin fly,' Jimbo complained.

The crippling drop in income with YoYo out of the band didn't help either, leaving behind two extra mouths to feed.

And the legal wranglings around whether charges would be laid, either first or second-degree murder, based on the jealous wife motive, led to a serious depletion of cash. Cash paid out to all the lawyers. Jimbo pleaded with them, 'How kin they charge someone fer bein stupid?' He even went so far as to try and shift the blame, 'It wuz that delibery guy what done it. He brung the wrong item to us, and poor Tambo knowed nuttin bout it.'

The police began to soften their stance, given the bizarre nature of the death, and considered the possibility of manslaughter or criminal negligence. Jimbo could have saved his breath. When his lawyers finally let the police interview Tambo, it became clear to them, with her three layers of make-up, polyester jumper, and bleach-blond hair all done up with a chiffon bow, that the poor woman didn't have it in her to arrange such a gruesome crime. With all the turmoil and drama, the band began to implode. There had been rumblings between the members that Jimbo had been going after this, that, and the other one. His hands and lips had been reaching out to the whole works of them, as it turned out. The cost of the bevy of lawyers for his defense against all the civil charges laid the whole thing to waste. The network TV and radio shows were wiped out in one fell swoop, not to mention leaving their reputation in tatters.

Tambo was too far gone to even listen to the griping and bellowing coming out of Jimbo. She was devastated that a simple error on her part had led to the demise of YoYo, lamenting that she could not have foreseen such a horrible event happening.

The turn in circumstances left Jimbo pondering the options for their future. A storm cloud followed him around as he fretted about what to do. He wasn't a master at hiding his emotions, and even though Jethro wasn't the sharpest knife in the drawer, he sensed it.

The idea of bolting crossed Jimbo's mind, leaving Tambo behind with the two boys. But he figured Tambo would make no sort of mother for them, always fretting over the fact that she had done their mother in. And not only that, she didn't have the time to raise them properly. She was a busy woman. Six hours a day shopping online, two hours primping and pampering herself to go out for a three-hour shopping spree, then stopping off at the Chick-a-Lickey-Lick or Big Bubba's Burstin Burger Joint to pick up supper. 'No,' he thought, 'I made me vows to her, and her alone. I'll have a little chat with me dearest-darlin.'

The next morning, he approached Tambo and said, 'I been doin just bout everthin, baby, but I cain't be abidin this sityebiation. No, no, I cain't be abidin it.'

'What the debil ya cryin bout now, Jimbo? Abidin what?' Tambo demanded.

'Those chilbren. Oh, look, I is so perturbulated I cain't eben talk right. I mean those children just cain't stay with us no more. We done near outta operatin cash, twisty Tambo.'

'I don't wanna hear another word bout that, Jimbo. All's I wanna know is iffin we got enough fer the next deelibery o make-up.'

'Yeah, yeah, sweet silliness, I done squirrellied away some investments in a place called the Caveman Islands, so we need to be headin there real soon-like. But we won't escape all this here mayhem if we is draggin those two youngins along with us.'

'You ain't tellin me we is gonna be livin in a cave, are ya

Jimbo?'

'No, we ain't gonna be doin that, butter biscuit. Don't you worry bout nuttin. I got it all figured out. The folks over there sound like a bunch o knuckle-draggers, and mayhaps we kin kick off a new Lordy show there.'

Jethro entered the room singing the latest hit tune from that handsome duo, Howlin Notes.

> ♫ Sleazy Jimmie's chilling….out of time
> When will he pop
> When will he swear he
> Will leave her slime
> She looks like Noddy
> But she makes him whole
> He don't care if she acts
> Like a troll ♫
> ♫ Aww, he won't leave that cat, ho, hoooo
> Won't pray alone ♫

Jimbo grabbed Jethro's meaty arm, hauled him aside, and whispered sternly, 'Lord thunderin! Ye singin bout me and Tambo there, Jethro? Those words ain't fit to be spoken.'

'Oh, no, Uncle Jimbo. It was just that funny Darlyn who made up some silly lyrics.'

Jimbo got control of himself and said, 'Emm, well, I don't wanna be hearin that flyin outta yer face agin. No, no, I can't go fer that a'tall. But listen up real good, handsome boy. Those two children gotta go, ain't no discussin bout it one way or t'other.'

'Dat be soundin right severe, big Jimbo. Whatcha gonna do with em?'

'I ain't gonna do nuttin, *you* is,' Jimbo said.

'I cain't take care o those two rascals, Jimbo!'

'You'll take care o em, alrighty, by droppin em off real early tomorra mornin at the address I'm gonna give ya.'

'Do I git to drive the hog-tied Lincoln agin?' Jethro asked.

'Yep, tall-boy, and ye kin have a right fine cruise in her fer the rest o the day, iffin ya want to.'

Jethro smiled expansively, 'Mmm-doggie, I is gonna have a right fine time doin that, generous Jimbo. You kin put that in yer pipe and take it to the bank!'

The next morning, Jimbo woke everyone up early and Tambo fed them a hearty breakfast of goose eggs Benedictine and grilled coot tails. While they were having breakfast, Tambo went to pack a small backpack for each of the boys. She struggled with the task, trying desperately to see through her tears, and worried about the severity of the blotching of her face. When they finished breakfast, they strapped the kids into the back seat of the Lincoln and as they wheeled away, Jimbo waved and said, 'Have a fun day!' And under his breath said, 'Ya little monsters.'

Jimbo wasted no time at all once they were out of the driveway. He and Tambo caught a limo to the airport for an early morning flight to the Caveman Islands.

Chapter 8 - Nazareth

Carmalita and her husband Mobie never started out together with much, except for a whole lot of lovin. It was a feeling that had been there in their households growing up, as divergent as those two environments were. His in the dirt-poor ethnic community of Shatnopoopoo, in the Great Territory of Tango Sea, and hers in the tiny black enclave in And-Courage, way up north in the Great Territory of I'll-Ask-Ya.

But now, Mobie just felt like he was drifting away, seemingly on a cloud, with Carmalita right there beside him. Both were so caught up in the sweet graces God gave them that they had to give something back, spread some joy around. They wanted to let everyone feel the love and help them overcome their wretched struggles brought on by the effects of segregation and underemployment.

They both worked hard, Carmalita at her low wage social justice advocacy firm, being admitted to the Bar five years earlier. And Mobie, running the local food bank and soup kitchen, singing at local gigs to fulfill his real passion. He had a gift but just couldn't seem to get the break he needed. If he ever did, he knew what he would do - feed more hungry people.

He would often try tunes out on Carmalita around the house, randomly singing new lyrics that would pop into his head. And Carmalita knew what to do, how to inspire him, urge him on. She would hear him working out the tune, humming it through, and then she would hit him with it, 'Let me give you some heat, boy, and free up your soul,' and she'd start clapping to the tune she heard him humming. Mobie would lay it down, feel it in his soul, indeed, so much so that it *would* free his soul. One day his break would come, they both knew it, and expected it to happen anytime soon.

What they didn't expect after they arrived and went into the food bank early one morning was to hear pounding on the door.

They had been inside setting things up in the hall when they heard it. Perplexed, Carmalita thought it might be an early client and went out to open the door. And there they stood, a six-year-old boy and what she assumed was his younger brother. They were just standing there all alone with not another soul in sight.

'Dear me, sweet babies, come in out of the rain. Where in heavens did you come from?' Carmalita asked the older one.

'Some loco guy by the name of Jethro dropped us off here a couple minutes ago,' the boy said.

She looked around outside but didn't see any vehicles around. 'Good Lord in heaven, that's the strangest thing. There's lots of guys go by that name around these parts. What's *your* name, son?'

'I'm Abe, and he be me little brother, Amos Moses,' Abe said as he pointed at Amos.

'Well, come on in. Are you hungry, would you like something to eat?' she asked as she studied Amos.

'Well, we had breakfast quite a piece ago afore we got in the car so, yeah, we's hungry.'

'Okay, we'll get you something, but first, where did you come from?'

Abe said, 'I dunno, ma'am. We drove for a long time though.'

'Who were you staying with before you came here, Abe?'

'I dunno,' he said, 'those folks had bout sixty-two nicknames fer each other what I couldn't never keep straight.'

Mobie came out to see what was going on and Carmalita explained the situation. He was perplexed too, not only by Amos' appearance, but hardly believing that two children were abandoned on their doorstep, so he asked Abe, 'Do you know what time you got in the car?'

'No,' Abe said, 'but it wuz dark.'

'Oh, goodness gracious,' Carmalita said, 'that must have been hours and hours ago.'

Abe shrugged his shoulders and said, 'Mayhaps.'

She invited the boys into the kitchen and got them some toast, back bacon, and each a glass of orange juice, and then said, 'You boys stay here and finish that up while Mobie and I talk over what to do, okay?'

'Sho as shootin, thank ye,' Abe said. Carmalita returned a smile and went out to the hall with Mobie.

'What are we going to do, Carmie? Boys that young abandoned by somebody from who knows where.'

Carmalita said, 'I know, it's odd, and so is the vibe I'm getting from the young one, Amos Moses. I guess we'll have to contact social services and see what they can do to sort this out. Not that I have much faith in *that* system these days, given what I see at work every day.'

'Yeah, I know what you mean both ways. That little fella has some kind of magnetic draw about him. Maybe it's got something to do with that odd ring of hair he has, it almost seems to glow. But anyway, let's see what you can find out and I'll keep them here for the day.'

'Okay Mobie. Let's finish setting up and after we run our errands, I'll make some calls from work.'

She went back into the kitchen to find the boys wrestling around on the floor. Abe appeared to be pretty rough with the little guy and she put a clamp on his shoulder, 'I'll have none of that, Abe. There will be no shenanigans like that around here, so don't push your luck, little fella. You hear me, right?'

'Yes ma'am, yes ma'am. Nobody ever told me I couldn't do that befo.'

'Well, I'm telling you now and I won't tell you again, if you know what I'm saying.'

Abe, thinking about her grip on his shoulder, looked at her fearfully and said, 'I do, I do, ma'am. I unnerstand altogether-like.'

She gave him the evil eye, 'Alright, you do as I say, or you'll be in big trouble. Mobie and I have to go uptown to meet Missy Roses and her crazy jester, Juke, so I want you to behave yourself.'

'I will, Miss Carmalita. Who be goin to take care o us when ye skedaddle uptown?'

'I have a friend coming over, her name is Franny, and she's bringing her dog. I'll be going to work later and I'll make some calls to find out what to do with the two of you. Franny can look after you here until we get things settled. You behave yourself while we're gone.'

'Yes ma'am, I sureliest will.'

At that moment, a Labrador Retriever bounded in through the door with Franny right behind it, and she called out, 'Good morning!' When she saw the children, she exclaimed, 'Goodness gracious, what do we have here?'

'Believe it or not, Franny, somebody dropped these two boys on the doorstep after we came in this morning. This one's name is Abe and the other one over there looking at the Bible stories is Amos,' Carmalita said.

Abe yelled out, 'Amos Moses, git yerself o'er here and see this big dog.' The dog growled at him but started wagging his tail when he saw Amos. Amos stumbled over at Abe's command and rubbed the dog's head. 'That be one big dog, Abe!' He looked around and asked, 'Do we get to feed him?'

Franny laughed, 'I didn't bring any food, but you can feed him from that can,' she said as she pointed to a can of dog food on the cupboard shelf.

Mobie, who overheard the conversation, piped in, 'Just hold on there, Franny, he seems a feastful dog.'

She said, 'No worries, Mobie, just give him an extra single can.'

The exchange reminded Mobie of a tune by The Band, a weighty song with dark lyrics. Lyrics that, unbeknownst to them at the moment, perfectly suited the situation they were currently in. He looked at Carmie and suddenly broke out into song.

♫ I'd take that boy of yours and I'd bring him on inside
Don't want Beelzebub to snatch him from our lives
But look, dear Carmie, don't let things go upside down

Just hide him over there, where we know he won't
be found ♫

Carmie laughed and they sang the chorus together, which was wont to happen from time to time.

♫ It don't bode well for Franny
Don't bode well for thee…eee
It don't bode well for many
Cause men (men) (men) ya know his code is an evil
creed (his code is an evil creed) ♫

Mobie finished off the ditty with another solo.

♫ Look at Amos Moses, I can tell he likes to play
He ain't no joke though, cause one day he might
join the fraa-aay
Hell, it all depends, if he can seem angelic and
lordlyyyy
And with that head of hair he's got, he's sure to be
a master of puppetry ♫

Carmie laughed and said, 'Strange how lyrics like that were written ten years ago and here we are now with a kid named in the song.'

Franny's brow furrowed. 'Hmm, odd indeed,' and she said.

Mobie piped up, 'Let's get going, Carmie. And Franny, we'll be back around ten. After that Carmie can make some calls to see what we can do with these boys.'

Carmalita waved on the way out and said, 'Toodle-oo for now, and you boys be good.' As she was closing the door she warned Franny to keep an eye on Abe's behavior.

Chapter 9 – Deliverance

For all the calls Carmalita made through her network of contacts in the justice system, no one could find out where the two boys came from. Day after day she was more confused, wanting to find them a good home, but becoming more and more attached to them.

The Social Services worker placed the boys in the Home for Motherless Children. It was a fine home indeed, run as it was by Quick Hands Eric, the fastest collard green chopper this side of the Mrs. Pippi River.

He employed the finest staff and made use of the most advanced techniques in child development. He offered outstanding artistic programs (primarily focused on the guitar and ukulele), and cooking classes (specializing in Opossum Stew and Tango Sea Mountain Stack Cakes). And the address was ideal, being so close to their home, just over at 461 Ocean Boulevard. Carmalita and Mobie could zip over anytime for a visit or take them out for the day.

The boys spent more time with Mobie than Carmalita, but they both noticed the way Amos was. After they dropped the boys off one night, Mobie said to her, 'I'll tell you, Carmie, there's something about that boy, Amos. I know he's just a kid, but he seems to have that "It" factor. You know, that intangible thing most of us wish we had that draws people to us.'

Carmalita agreed, 'Yes, and that's in spite of his lisp. And now that I think of it, I hardly notice it at all anymore.'

'Ha, me too,' Mobie said, 'and with his charisma, or whatever you call it, he might go a lot farther than people give him credit for.'

'I think you're right, Mobie.' She thought about the situation and said, 'You know, I think Amos has the potential to be a good boy, but I'm not so sure about Abe. They're brothers, so they need to stay together, but Abe could be a bad influence on him.'

'I agree, but what can we do about it?' Mobie asked.

'What do you say we take them in. That way we can try to get Abe straightened away and Amos should be fine. God knows the boy will need a lot of help.'

Mobie thought about it and asked her, 'What about the practicalities of it? How would we arrange everything, timewise I mean?'

Carmalita said, 'Like everything else, I suppose. We'd just have to make a schedule. Maybe you could take care of them at the food bank through the day, and I could care for them at night when you score a gig.'

'That sounds good to me, Mamalita, if Social Services will let us.'

Carmalita smiled, 'Mamalita, you said? I kind of like that, Mobie.'

Mobie grinned, 'You've always been my sweet Mamalita, Carmalita.'

She laughed, 'Well, it's only fostering, so they should agree to it. It would help the kids out and take some burden off the system, too.'

'Sounds like a win-win situation when you put it that way, lovin baby.'

They both smiled and headed off to bed, happy that they were going to have a family, as odd as it seemed. When Mobie laid his head down on the pillow, he began to think it over. He wouldn't let the boys succumb to a fate like that, being raised in a "group home". He knew through personal experience, having lost his father early in life, what it was like not to be in a home with two parents to look after and guide a youngster. The HMC was a fine facility, and even though Quick Hands Eric was an awesome role model, lately he seemed to be a bit lazy and living in an alternate time. At least that's what his girlfriend had been saying around town. He snuggled up to Carmalita and told her what he had been thinking.

'I agree, Mobie. Children should be under one roof with two parents. And I've heard rumors around town that are a bit disturbing. I overheard Eric's mama talking about him, too. Calling him crazy, saying he wanted to go into the movies. That sound's odd since he already has a fine, in fact illustrious, career.'

For Mobie, the discussion made him think about the lyrics of the latest chart-topping single, "Given My Pulse Is Fine", by a singer out of Tulsa, Cleric Captain, and he began to softly sing.

> ♫ Given my pulse is fine
> Given my pulse is fine
> Don't know how I'll do it
> But I know I gotta do it
> Gotta get outta this slime ♫

> ♫ So, here I be where I never should
> Knowin I gotta get outta this hood
> Walkin down the out-of-time line
> I'll swear I got the cooties
> Thought I seen em in my thong
> Seems I'z only chasin slime ♫

Carmalita smiled at Mobie, and he winked and whispered to her, 'Oh, yeah, I've heard all those stories about him. And it won't be like that for those boys. They'll be staying with us.'

***

Try as they did, Moby and Carmalita never did get Amos on the right track. He did well enough with his marks in school to get by but spent most of his time listening to Jazz. Mostly Miles Davis. He did have one friend, or more like acquaintance, by the name of Allbliss that he talked about occasionally, but he seemed to be a bit of a loner. And Abe, forget about it. He was as wild and unruly as they came. He behaved when they were there to keep him in check, but he was a sneaky little devil, forever scheming and conjuring up some sort of trouble. But he was good to Amos, and that's what mattered most. The poor boy desperately needed a helping hand, someone who believed in him, saw his value, and Abe was there for him. No matter how many times Amos fell, Abe would be waiting to catch him, time after time.

So the four of them, like any family, got through it all, with Abe heading for High School and Amos in Junior High. An odd family, for sure, Carmalita thought, but what family isn't?

Chapter 10 - Amos Meets His Pappy

At the impressionable age of sixteen while trudging along home, alone as usual, Amos came upon a store that had flames shooting out of the windows, a record store in fact, and heard someone screaming from inside. He dashed into the store and managed to drag a man across the street to safety. Amos offered him a drink of water and asked, 'Are you okay, mithter?'

The man took a drink from the bottle and said, 'I think so. Thanks fer gettin me out of there, kiddo.'

A rubbernecker slowly approached with his car window rolled down, wanting to see what was going on. He had an 8-track tape playing a song by The Hoo at full volume, which was astonishingly appropriate given that Amos and the store owner, Theo, didn't know who was who. Call it Karma.

♫ Boooo hoo-hoo…hoo-hoo hoo-hoo
   Yer marijuana went aglow
   Boooo hoo-hoo…hoo-hoo hoo-hoo
   Yer sad today and full of woe
   Boooo hoo-hoo…hoo-hoo hoo-hoo ♫
♫ Boooo hoo-hoo…hoo-hoo hoo-hoo
   Oh no, I think she's gonna blow
   Boooo hoo-hoo…hoo-hoo hoo-hoo
   Looks like we're gonna see a show ♫

As the driver continued down the street, the building exploded into a towering inferno of sparks, vinyl, and recording tape. Sweet smelling smoke began wafting through the air, with the street beginning to look like a New Year's Eve celebration in Times Square. The neighbors were never a happier lot, including the local convenience store owner, who ran out of every type of munchie on the shelves.

Theo groaned and rolled over. He dusted himself off, and then looked up at the young boy who had saved him, 'Who is ye, son?'

'Amoth, Amoth Motheth,' he said, as spittle flew from his mouth into the face of the man.

'Jesus, son. You don't have to do that. It's not like I is on fire or anything like that.'

'Thorry, mithter, thorry about that,' as another eruption of fluid shot forth from his mouth.

The man wiped his face again and eyed Amos up and down, taking note of his wandering eyes and odd ring of blond hair encircling his head. 'What kind of creature is this?' he wondered. It might have been the sixteen years since he last saw the child, or maybe the endless succession of inventions in the illicit drug industry, or more likely a combination of the two, that fogged his memory, but there was something familiar about the boy. A spark of recognition; a bus, a long skinny newborn with a little donut of hair, and eyes like that, ones that made the hair on the back of his neck stand up.

He squinted and thought, 'So, he's back, growed up tall now, and as sure as shootin that's the little devil who popped out of that sweet young cellist on the bus that day.'

Amos decided to hang around until the fire brigade arrived to douse the flames and the paramedics checked the man over for injuries. When Theo went over to thank Amos again, Amos asked, 'Ith that your thtore that burnt?'

The man said, 'One o em. I got a chain o em all o'er Tango Sea. Mayhaps you done heard bout em, Theodopolus's Pop-Odopolus World. They're music stores and I carry every pop hit that wuz ever produced. My name's Theo, by the way.'

'Wow, that ith awethome, Theo By-the-way. I'd love to work at a place like that. I love muthic, ethpethially Jazz.'

'Well son, just call me Theo, okay, but you won't be working at this one.' Amos laughed uncontrollably at what he thought was a joke, and Theo started to think that this kid was about as sharp as a bowling ball. Which led him to think that he might be a good candidate for a below-minimum-wage position in the newly rebuilt store. He said to Amos, 'But mayhaps when it's fixed up, I might have some work fer ya, ya know, get ya set on the ko-rrect path in life.'

'Wow, that would be awethome, Mithter Theo!'

Theo ducked just in time to avoid the spray. 'Now don't git yer knickers all knotted up, young feller. And ya kin ditch the Mister part hence wise, just Theo will do.'

'Okee-dokee, Theo-will-do.'

'Oh, no, no! I be spellin it fer ya now, so listen up hard and true. It's T-H-E-O. Got it now?'

'Yeth, I think I do, Theo.'

'Good, now listen up, and listen up good. I'm not the most certainest I kin put ya out on the floor with the customers, given, emmhmm, yer, uh, yer condition, shall I say.'

'Whatcha mean by that, Theo. Me brother Abe been thayin I wuz born perfect, in me own handthome thtyle, and I otta keep me head held up high ath kin be.'

'I is truly sorry, sonny-bubbles, but mayhaps iffin ya wear some type o contraption, like a sneeze-guard or sumpin, I could put ya out on the floor with the customers.'

'Ye won't regret keepin me outta hidin, Theo,' Amos said.

'Mayhaps not, Amos. But remember what I'm sayin now. I cain't afford any lawsuits from customers who got hit in the eye by a little bitty kernel o sumpin flyin outta yer yapper.'

'Okay, Theo. I'll be on the lookout fer one o them thar thingth ya mentioned, that thneeze-guard contraption.'

'Sure, sure thing, sonny. You do that.' Theo wasn't so much interested in building a relationship with his son as he was in employing cheap labor, and he thought there might be another benefit to getting close to Amos. The kid's mother was a fine cellist indeed, and Theo hoped she might have done well for herself. Always on the lookout for an extra dollar or two, he planned to find out what became of her, or more accurately, how much money she had. Dealing drugs out of the back of his stores was getting dangerous, and he had been thinking it was time to go into a less risky line of work. Little did he know what this new relationship would lead to.

The job didn't pay much, but Amos didn't care about that. He was in his glory working in Theo's record store sorting albums and trying his best to serve customers. After several days, Theo noticed the revulsion on many of his customers faces after an exchange with Amos, brought on by Amos' constant ejection of spittle into his face shield. He thought it prudent to insist that Amos wear a mask instead and Amos was ecstatic when Theo gave him one with the Rolling Stones red tongue emblazoned on the front, as the color matched his MAGA hat perfectly.

Carmalita and Mobie were thrilled that Amos was working part-time and loved his job. They thought the store looked a little shady, but like most parents, they were happy if he was happy. Abe took up a position at the store too, but they quickly lost track of him when he moved out right after high school and, truth be told, were kind of glad of it. They did know, from what Amos told them, that Abe was still a big help to him, but there was no denying it, he was trouble.

The two boys eventually found out about their paternity, but Theo insisted their relationship remain a secret. While they both happily worked at the store helping their father, Abe, being a true chip off the old block, pulled one con after another. But Amos, all unawares of Abe's crooked behavior, looked up to and adored him.

Theo adored something, too, and it surely wasn't Abe. It was low hanging fruit, the kind that nobody noticed when an exchange was made. For Theo, what he liked was the type of cash rolling in where he could remain anonymous, selling soft-core drugs to people the cops wouldn't bother with. He had always run his products through the well-to-do Ivy League types. They'd come in to get their albums and then score a "personal use" bag of this or that, maybe even a bit extra to sell to their buddies.

The troubles that that little bulldog Abe created for Theo were endless, skimming off product or inflating prices and pocketing the difference. When Abe wanted to branch out and "expand the product line", Theo put his foot down.

He told Abe, 'Listen sonny, ye'd be gettin into too much risky stuff with what yer yackin bout. I got meself a nice tidy business as it is, with no trouble just as things be. I won't be havin any o that Exyasee and Bendyertill floatin around me place.'

'Ha, funny one there, pappy. It's Ecstasy and Fentanyl, but I like yer take on it, cause this stuff'll surely bend yer till, hahaha.'

'I be tellin ya, Abe. Don't let me catch ya messin round with that thar stuff, or ye might get stuffed yer ownself.'

'Oh, Theo-poppin-less, yer getting too old fer this business,' Abe said. 'Ye gotta keep up with the times cause I tell ya, the times, they is a changin.'

Theo whacked Abe upside the head and said, 'I'll only say it once again, Abe. Don't ya be bringin any more o those gangs or strollin ladies roundbout me stores no more, or ya just might find yerself on t'other side o tomorrow.'

He let the issue go at that because he had bigger fish to fry at the moment. He noticed how his customers were drawn to Amos, for some ungodly reason, and he began to think that Amos just might be his meal ticket. Call it a sixth sense, or perhaps a sick sense, but he thought there was some juice to be squeezed out of that boy. And he was bound and determined to find out how to capitalize on the opportunity.

So, Theo had the cash and Amos had, well, not much of anything. But Theo wanted to get things moving for his son and promptly set the wheels in motion.

Time and again Amos had invited one of his classmates, Allbliss, over to the shop, and Theo noticed something in the boy. He was a bit of a twitchy little critter with his knees always knockin about and hips a-swivelin to and fro, but he seemed to have his wits about him, did well in school, too. And he was a handsome devil, or so all the girls he brought around thought.

The opportunity was evident to Theo, and he jumped at

the chance to get Amos' head straightened out, get him some business sense. 'Amos, ya otta get yerself into college and learn how business works, like the accountin stuff. Then you kin help me out with all me money. Things is heatin up businesswise, ya know.'

'Ya really think I thhould do that, Pappy?'

'Yep, son. It would do you a pile o good to get some smarts into yerself.'

'Well, Pappy, I'm not thure if my markth ith good enough to git in anywhere.'

'Don't ye worry yo head bout that, youngin. I got a plan, and ain't none o me plans ever failed me so far in this scandalous life.'

'Okay, Pappy, what e'er you thay thoundth good to me.'

Two days later Allbliss appeared at the store and Theo took him aside. 'Listen, knocky-knees, I need ya to take Amos' SAT exams fer him so he kin git hisself into college.'

Allbliss, sensing an opportunity, responded, 'That sounds kind of risky to me, Mister Theo. What if I get caught?'

'I already pondered that question, boy. We'll keep it all secret-like, and I'll set ye up just as pretty as that handsome face ye be wearin.'

'I might take that on faith, Mister Theo, but how about this, just to be sure. I'll hold off on fixing up that exam until I see my full college tuition's been paid for.'

Theo reluctantly agreed, 'That be a ton o cash, ya little swindler, er, swiveler, but I guess we got a deal. I'll git on that quicker than you kin say Bob's yer uncle.'

***

Amos did well enough in college and so did Allbliss. The cash from Theo kept them afloat and Amos' marks put him into the top ten percentile, with some clever assistance from Allbliss.

When Abe pulled up at the campus in his Jeep to pick up Amos, he climbed in and said, 'Hey, Abe, they want me to give the keynote addrethth at the convocation ceremony. What in the world ith I gonna talk about?'

Being quick on the uptake, just like his old man, Abe grinned. 'Hey, buddy. Here's yer first chance to show those mucky-mucks you ain't just been whistlin dixie, if ya know what I mean.'

'No, big brother, I don't. Whatcha talkin about?'

'Well,' Abe said, 'all the talk these days is bout respectin people's *differences*. And like I told ya afore, I always got yer back cause ye is one special dude, so I'll tell ya what ya otta do. Those folks all like to cry and carry on like there's no tomorrow about every sad story, so lay it on thick and fast just what it's like to be *special* like yerself.'

So that's what Amos did. With Theo lurking at the back of the auditorium, he walked up onto the stage with his head held high (below his MAGA hat) and told his sad life's story of losing his mother (and that he didn't know how), about being taunted for his "unusual appearance", as he put it, and then finding his long-lost father. Half the class were in tears when he wrapped up his speech in dramatic fashion, 'Mayhapth there ain't no better motivator than revenge, cause I learned em all that there'th more to me than meetth the eye!'

The class loved it and gave him a standing ovation. When the graduates had their degrees in hand and had tossed off their caps, Amos was swarmed by the lot of them asking for his autograph. That was the point at which Theo confirmed what he felt about Amos, people gravitated to him.

It wasn't exactly his charisma, and it wasn't exactly sympathy, but something in between. Maybe it was his naiveté that helped bridge the gap for people, something like a loveable, endearing mascot for a team that could never win. You couldn't *not* want to either cuddle him or stick up for him. Whatever it was about Amos, Theo was, if nothing else, a master at spotting useful traits in people. Traits he could make use of himself, and he thought, 'I swear, that boy is gonna be a cash cow fer me, somehow or t'other'.

Struggling through the grind with work and family, Carmalita climbed the ladder in the justice department, first as a Public Defender, defending the people she had previously helped navigate the system. As a PD she was brilliant, managing to get many of her clients the help they needed, rather than them being sent off to Juvie or the Big House. And then as a Public Prosecutor she took the same approach, pleading out deals that would improve the outcomes for everyone, striking agreements that contained some semblance of retribution, but also provided for healthy measures of rehabilitation. She knew one thing that was paramount in all the cases – preserve the dignity of everyone involved, perpetrator and victim alike.

She gained quite a reputation during her twenty odd years of service, moving up through the ranks and grasping the reins of Tango Sea's Territorial Attorney General's Office. It was the most unusual set of circumstances that led to her unexpected rise to the Governor's post. The territory had been leaning slightly left of center after decades of right-wing rule. The Governor, Silly Jay Psoriasis, who only got voted into office on the strength of his one highly commercialized hit song, had died, ironically, of a broken heart after his daughter, Smiley, produced a series of hit albums that completely stole the limelight from him.

Being next in line to take over the Governorship, according to Territorial law, Carmalita gladly stepped into the role. Her commitment to change and the well-being of her citizens made national headlines and did not go unnoticed throughout the rest of the Great Union of Territories, particularly in the highest seats of power in the northeast.

The President of GUT, Baroque *Oh*-Mama, invited her to the Rainbow House for an evening meeting in the Trapezoidal Office. After he greeted her, he said, 'We need to talk, Carmalita. Just wait a minute.'

She gave him an uncomprehending look and wondered why he hadn't offered her a seat.

Baroque turned the lights down low and continued, 'We have two years left until the next GUT election and my two terms will be up.'

'What do you have in mind, sir?' she asked.

The President, throughout his life, was an affable and animated man when he spoke, just as he did now, 'I think our party needs a strong hand to lead this fractured union, and I also think it's about time we had a woman take over leadership of the territories.' He did a little shake of his hips and then a pirouette, the very kind of thing that endeared him to the voters.

'Well, Baroque, you think I'm the one for that role?'

'That's exactly what I think, Carmie, if I can call you that.'

'Yes sir, of course. And I'd be honored to run for the leadership. I'm not sure I can fill your shoes, though,' she noted with some concern.

'You have the credentials, Carmie, you just need a little act. That's what the folks are looking for these days. Listen, I've heard that some folks call you Mamalita, right?'

'Yes, my sons and a few friends do, sir.'

'So how good is that? You've got something to work with already.'

'What do you mean, Baroque?' she asked.

'You've heard that new song, Mama Mia?'

'Yes, of course. It's a huge hit,' she said.

'I know, and I can tell it will be popular for years to come. I'll even bet they'll make a musical out of it, play it on Broadway, too. You could play off that with the Mamalita angle, you know.' Baroque tried to recall, 'How does it go now, something like this?' and he began to sing.

> ♫ Mamalita, you're in the game to win
> Fly high, you have got the true view
> Mamalita, play the show to win
> Why, why, they'll bow down and kiss you ♫

♫ Well, you're just getting started
True....and highly regarded
Well, well, they all just love you so
Mamalita, I truly bet they'll go
We, we, we just all love ya so ♫

Carmalita said to him, 'Well, I don't know if that's exactly how the song goes, sir, but I would hope to have my policies be the important part of a run for the presidency.'

'They can be, Carmie, but you still need something catchy to hook the voters. You don't have to play the queen, but there's nothing wrong with doing a bit of dancing.' Baroque did a little twirl and nearly lost his balance before Carmalita caught him.

'Easy, sir,' she cautioned him.

'Yes, I know. At seventy-seven years old I'm just not as spry as I used to be. But listen, at your rallies why not have a jamboree, with lots of music. Convince everyone to take a chance on you, give them the time of their lives and they'll respond.'

'You're putting me in the mood, Baroque. Makes me feel like I'm seventeen again. And I'll take all of that under advisement. I'll just watch and see, what happens I mean.'

'Well, Mamalita, don't wait too long. Two years goes by fast and if you want to take a run at it, it'll have to start soon.'

'Okay, sir. I'll talk to Mobie. Give me a couple of weeks and I'll let you know what we decide.'

Baroque decided to dispense with the twirl and did a shiver and shake, with his arms protruding out to the sides, all the better to keep his balance. He grinned at her and said, 'I'll look forward to hearing back from you, Mamalita!'

Chapter 13 - Abe Skates On Thin Ice

Showing Amos the ropes in the legitimate side of the business, while trying to hide the other stuff, took a lot of Theo's time. But Amos was nobody's fool, having grown up with Abe. He now knew where all the 'loose cash' was coming from that was in Theo's safe. He explained to Theo that he wanted to put the money to use, so Theo gave him the contact information of a Rasputinskian ex-pat who he thought might be able to help put the money "into circulation". Amos got the money moving and in no time he expanded the number of stores and branched out into CDs, videos, and merchandise. Theo was impressed and decided to start his own YouTube channel with Amos doing cameo appearances, increasing his profile and following. He didn't know yet why he was doing it or to what end, but he still had a suspicion something big might come of the boy, even beyond the serious cash they were now raking in.

The increase in Amos' public image wasn't lost on Allbliss, and he took note of the expansion of the business. Within months Amos had half a million followers on the channel and even more on his Twitter account. He realized he should play off Amos' growing fame and, wanting to take advantage of the opportunity, approached him. 'Hey, Aiming-Amos, looks like you're aiming for the stars with all the chatter you're stirring up on social media these days.'

'Thingth ith crazy, no doubtin it, good buddy,' Amos said.

Allbliss took his chance, and he had an irresistible hook to reel Amos in, 'Do you think maybe I could perform a few songs on your channel once in a while? I could ask some of my dancing-girl fans to come on and add some spice to the act. I know Sharon would love to do it with her girlfriends.'

'Do you mean that gal Thharon I met afore with ya, Ali-B?'

'Yep, Sharon Share-alike is what she goes by.' He elbowed Amos in the ribs and winked, 'I'll get you a ticket for my next show and you can get to know her better there. The show is at Granny's Bold Yodellin House and it's going to be a good one.'

'Wow, I heard that ith a hot thpot, but I never been there afore.'

'It's hot alright, Amos, and it might get hotter with you and her there together.'

'What are ya thayin, Ali-B, I thought Thharon liked you?'

'That's exactly what I'm saying, Amos,' Allbliss grinned, 'she likes us both. I wrote this song for her.' He whispered to Amos, 'Stole the melody from Cranky Valley and The Core Reasons.' He started off in a high-pitched voice.

> ♫ Shaaaron (Sharon lady)
> Shaaaron (Sharon lady)
> Shaaaron, will you dress in your tights
> (dress, dress, dress in your tights) ♫

> ♫ Shaaaron (Sharon lady)
> Shaaaron (Sharon lady)
> Shaaaron, will you give some delights
> (some, some, some of your delights) ♫

Amos started giggling uncontrollably and Allbliss laughed, 'That should get her all worked up, don't you think?'

Amos got himself under control and said, 'Yeth, yeth, indeed it will!'

So, Amos went to the show and invited Abe along, who wanted to see what all the hype was about. He watched, none too happily, from the side-lines as Amos hit it off big time with Sharon while Allbliss enthralled the dancing girls in the audience.

And Abe, not used to being a bench-warmer, found it hard to contain himself, seeing Allbliss getting so much exposure on the YouTube channel performing skits and cover songs.

Allbliss' strong suit was his looks more than it was penning successful songs, so he didn't have a hit yet, but he did have lots of hits. His new followers, especially the girls, were agog with the way he wiggled and waggled around. Even though he was only playing cover tunes, all the bars and clubs were after him. He was playing more gigs than ever and getting more girls than ever, too.

Abe knew he would have to turn Amos around. Allbliss was getting too close to Amos and becoming his primary influencer, usurping Abe's standing with Amos. First it was the schooling, then it was sharing an apartment, and now it was the girls. Amos, who Abe always had under his wing, was branching out, becoming his own man, connecting with other people, and getting his kicks elsewhere.

For all he did to reel Amos back in, it never worked. First, he took him to his favorite bar and tried to ply him with booze, but Amos didn't like that. Amos was used to his wandering eyes, but he sure didn't like it when they started to spin around in opposite directions. No, Amos didn't like that feeling at all.

Next, Abe rolled up some funny stuff and gave Amos a few puffs. It turned out that neither one of them thought that was such a good idea. When Amos took a haul, he began to cough and gag, spewing forth more moisture than a tidal wave. Abe, who was sitting across from him, was in the direct line of fire and in the unfortunate position of not having his handkerchief at the ready.

His next move was ill advised, too. Amos was on a high, literally, so they left the bar and went next door to the casino to play some roulette. Abe knew the casino used left-handed roulette tables, which he thought would be perfect for Amos, since he was left-handed. Several problems arose out of this, though. Firstly, Amos' eyes tended to google to the left, but being confronted with a left-handed table meant the wheel itself spun to the right, while the ball rolled to the left. This was confusing enough, but what came next sent him into his own spin.

Not having played that casino in some time, Abe was not aware that a new dealer, who was trained in the European style of alternating the spin of the wheel on each turn, was running the wheel. This threw Amos into a deeper spin, with his left eye googling in one direction while his right eye was googling in another. Alas, he had to be carried out by security after he had a hard crash to the floor.

When they were outside the casino, Abe was worried that Amos' eyes weren't wandering around anymore, so he took him to the hospital. They kept him overnight for observation and Abe collected him the next morning, with no apparent damage done. Truth be told, Abe was more concerned about his failed attempts at getting Amos back onside than he was about his health. He knew who his meal ticket was, and he wasn't going to let it go so easily to that twisty Allbliss.

***

As usual, Theo had his ear to the ground and knew what was going on. With the designs he had on Amos himself, he didn't much like all the double-usurping he was hearing about. First there was Abe, then there was Allbliss, and now Abe at war with Allbliss, making a spectacle of themselves all about town. No, that wouldn't do. Theo liked things to be low-key, staying in the shadows.

All that was bad enough but add to it everything else attributable to Abe; the missing cash, the missing stash, the cars he crashed, not to mention his lack of class, Theo was at his wits end. 'Surprising,' he thought, 'the wicked little devil wasn't nicknamed Bobby Bass.'

And then there were the gangs, pimps, and hookers who kept coming around. No, Abe hadn't heeded Theo's warning at all, brushing it off as just a feeble threat from an old man who didn't have it in him to keep up with the evolving market.

The unfortunate part of it was, at least for Abe, Theo did have some remaining wits about him.

Sadly, for Abe, as shifty as he was, his father was shiftier. Yes, Theo knew Abe would take a turn at some point and rise up against him, try some more usurping and try to steal the wealth he had amassed. He knew by now that Amos was his ticket to ride, and he wasn't about to let Abe get in the way of it.

The record business was universal, and Theo's contacts were, too. He was shipping albums, well, goods of some sort or other, worldwide. The market in Rasputinskia had been hot for a few years now, and Theo was riding the wave, shipping them heavy volumes of vinyl, and whatever else they craved, on a weekly basis. He was a perceptive guy, and he soon noticed a "consolidation" in the Rasputinskian market. One after the other, the Rasputinskian distributors "fell away", leaving him one point of contact for his shipments.

Being a man of many talents, one of which was possessing an expertise in saving his own ass, he knew what he needed to do. He would take care of that goon Abe, who he was sure was going to land him in jail, or more than likely six feet under, sooner or later.

Theo learned through his contacts that the Rasputinskians had a long history of expertise in the art of subterfuge. They employed the most ingenious methods imaginable of "consolidation", some so downright unbelievable that people could only assume that the incidents must have been accidental.

After communicating with his Rasputinskian contact, Theo decided on a plan of action. The preferred method for Abe's removal included a classic blame-shift and was the one he selected.

Early one morning Theo approached Abe and told him, 'Hey Abe, I got a packet I need to get to a customer right away. Run it over to him. It's just a mile down, over on Tenth Avenue.'

'What's in it fer me, so-so-Theo?'

'How long have I been tellin ya not to call me that, ya two-bit mugger!'

Abe laughed, 'Fifty days, ya old fat bugger.'

Theo said, 'Ha, kinda reminds me o a song I heard once by that little guy, what's his name, Saul Rhymin. How'd it go? Oh, mayhaps like this.'

> ♫ Well, nip down the track, ya hack
> And take this to the man, man
> Do it with joy, boy
> Don't even stop fer a pee ♫

> ♫ Drop all yer lust, just
> Don't get yerself nonplussed
> And give him the kilos, see
> Then bring the money to me ♫

He stopped singing and came to his senses. 'Now, get this over there pronto. I'll give you a six-pack when you get back.' Theo handed the packet to Abe and he happily left, looking forward to his early morning refreshments to come.

When he stepped out into the rain he pulled up his hoodie. He had only travelled a few blocks when he was held up by a red light. While taking it easy, standing on the corner of Winslow and Arizona, he thought about doing Theo in and began singing The Giggles latest hit, more or less, waiting for the light to change.

> ♫ Thinkin he's cheesy, thinkin he's cheesy
> That Theo's mounds of high school deals
> Are all so sleazy
> Sell them crack if you're a man
> Won't even care if it is banned
> Must sell it out, he can be damned
> And get rid of cheesy ♫

He was interrupted when he heard a thunderous crash behind him. The streets and sidewalks were unusually barren, with not a car or pedestrian to be seen. He turned to see what the racket was and noticed that a flat-bed Ford had lost its load. He was immediately mesmerized by what had fallen off the back of the truck and escaped its cage. It was upon him in an instant, a six-hundred-pound flash of orange and black-striped fur.

According to the autopsy report, considering the few toes and little amount of sinew and bones that were left on the street, more likely than not it had been a Siberian tiger, with four-inch canines and a bite Dracula would have envied. No one saw it come and no one saw it go, but everyone knew that Rootin Tootin Moe Neurotic from over in the neighboring territory was a loose cannon, not only with his mouth and firearms, but with the way he transported his terrifying felines.

The public were agog, and the media outlets' headlines had a field day with the story. "It was a Tiger Thing!" – "Four Toes Moe?" – "Shere Khan-sumption!"

Not a thing could be proven though, since Moe had been out of the territory looking for that bitch he hated so much, Feral Bastard. And who cared anyway? The victim was just another two-bit hustler in a long line of con men throughout the territory, some who had certainly suffered more torturous fates than Abe.

One, for instance, was known to have been tied up, both hands and feet, and zipped into a body bag along with a lightly tranquilized boa constrictor. Many said it looked like the work of a Rasputinskian operative who went by the name of Krushin Krushelniski. Most just thought that was exactly what the victim had coming.

In another particularly gruesome death.....ohh, let's not go there.

Amos, none the wiser to what Theo had done, turned to his father for solace, trying to understand how he would get through life without Abe's support. Carmalita and Mobie were devastated that Amos had lost his older brother, but that was about as far as it went.

At the memorial service, Mobie wiped the tears from Carmalita's face and whispered, 'I hate to say it, but the world probably is a better place without him in it.'

Carmalita nodded, and then cried some more.

Chapter 15 - Amos Gets His Groove On

The consequences of what he had done never occurred to Theo. He'd never put any thought into that. He had risen from a gamblin man way down south out of Two-Animes, Squeezie-Anna, to make a pretty good life for himself. Back in the old days he was only satisfied when he was on a drunk. But now, having arranged his own son's death, it quite unexpectedly got to him, made him feel like he was wearing a ball and chain. He desperately needed someone to talk to, and it didn't take him long to get reacquainted with one of his old friends, Jim, Jim Beam. Amos shared Theo's grief but was surprised how hard he'd hit the bottle. Through all those years watching Abe's double-dealing, Amos was wise enough to recognize the opportunity at hand.

The suggestion Amos put forward intrigued Theo, a much-deserved vacation. Maybe go back to his house in Two-Animes for a few months and ponder his future. Theo liked the idea and felt relieved when he cracked open yet another bottle.

Three hours later, the time to strike was nigh, and Amos took his shot. He convinced Theo to make him a full partner in the business. On the day of the signing, Theo was more than half in the bag. Amos strolled into the boardroom with his MAGA hat on and, when the lawyer collected the signed contract - Amos Moses, Senior Partner - Theo Dopolis, Junior Advisor - Amos handed the bag of cash under the table to the lawyer. Theo never suspected Amos in the least and promptly headed down south for some R and R.

When Amos took the reins of power, the first item on his agenda was to get his lisp corrected. He thought it miraculous that he was able to control his lisping after several intensive sessions with a speech pathologist. Given that success, he decided to get hair implants (a combination of blond on blond), which had an astonishing side effect. The weekly medication he had to take to keep his hair implants stable also corrected his wandering eyes.

***

When Allbliss returned from an extended road show and met Amos at the store, he was amazed at his transformation. Over a drink of Sarsaparilla, Allbliss thought he might capitalize on the potential in front of him, so he suggested, 'Look Amos, why are we working so hard?'

'We be just takin care o business, every day, Ali-B.'

'Yeah,' Allbliss said, 'we're takin care of business alright, and working overtime to do it. Taking that god-awful train every morning, trying to get in before nine. And then if the train is late, mercy me! Managing sixteen stores, running around day and night all over hell's half-acre to sort out every little problem that comes up. We never get to laze around in the sun, you know, be mellow and work at nothing all day.'

'Whatcha thinkin bout doin, Ali-B? We need to be makin some money, and no one else is gonna do it fer us.'

'That's where you're wrong, good buddy. Everything these days is branding and franchising. With your handsome new look, you should sell these stores off and focus on marketing the brand, with you as the mascot, or whatever you call it. Let the other guys take care of their stores and we take a piece of their action.' The thought of all that money reminded Allbliss of one of his favorite Stink Freud songs and he began to sing and swivel about.

> ♫ Honey…let's attack
> We's…just…fine Mac
> We'll take a piece of their sack ♫
> ♫ Honee-ee-ee-ey…take a bit
> Just take every penny we can get
> We'll be the sly-prosperity low-crass groveling duet
> So, let's get ourselves set ♫

62

Amos gave Allbliss a quizzical glance, 'Them thar lyrics ain't soundin like I remember em from the song, Ali-B.'

'Maybe they're not, Amos, but they're right as rain for what I am trying to tell you.'

His motive didn't involve making more money. All he wanted to do was sing, and as things were, he didn't have enough time for that. He had some local name recognition but expanding operations into some of the neighboring territories would give him a wider base to draw on. That was the key, he needed to play to a bigger base, and he needed a better brand name behind him. Theodopolous's Pop-Odopolus Music World just wouldn't do.

Amos shook his head, 'I don't know, Ali-B. We got things nice and fine as they is, and it sounds risky to me.'

'Well Amos,' Allbliss said, 'you always said you wanted to prove what you have in you. So far, you just took over some stores, and that's about it, no disrespect intended, good buddy. If you want to really stand out in life you need to take some risks. And believe me, I know it. My knees are taking an awful pounding, but it's a hook I sure hope pays off someday soon.'

Amos looked at him for a full minute before he said, 'I never thought about that. I do like the plan, alright. And that's what all the schoolin was talkin about, brandin and franchisin. Iffin ya really think I got the looks fer it, mayhaps I should go fer it.'

Allbliss did a little waggle of his shoulders and sang out, 'It's now or never, I'm telling you; this thing won't waaaait.'

Amos smiled and said, 'Okay, Ali-B, I'll go to the bank and ask them fer a loan to git er done.'

***

With the financing secured, Amos expanded into other territories, creating his "Brand" and implementing a franchising model. At Allbliss' urging, given their shared love of jazz and their idolatry of Miles Davis, they settled on a new name – Towering Trumpets.

The timing couldn't have been better, it was the glory

days of music, with business expanding at breakneck speed. He refurbished the Dimwit Sellers building in downtown Nachoville, Tango Sea, which he got for a steal with the loan from the bank. The previous owners, who were not known for their marketing skills, had pumped all their hopes and money into production, sales, and installation of living room in-floor shuffleboards. Unsurprisingly, they vacated the building after a few short months.

It was a brilliant move on Amos' part, buying the century-old two-storey building and adding two floors above. Allbliss woo-ed the city council with his mesmerizing hip-swiveling, which helped Amos get around the zoning by-laws and, well, the issue of the historical artifacts that were destroyed in the process of refurbishing the building.

The naming of it was a stroke of genius too, unveiling it at the ribbon-cutting ceremony as Trumpeting Tower. So, Amos had his flagship building with Jazz on the first floor, Rock and Roll on the second, Rhythm and Blues on the third, and then a little pet project of his on the fourth floor – bands doing re-makes of songs using misheard lyrics.

The franchises sprung up over many of the southern territories, with Amos the face of the brand. It might have seemed an unusual choice, but by adding dark sunglasses (selected from the Roy Orbital line) to his image make-over, Amos pulled it off.

Chapter 16 – Theo Gets Voted Off The Island

'Amoth Motheth,' Theo mumbled to himself through his drunken stupor, 'ya really made a go of it, didn't ya. Grew the buthinethth like nobody's buthinethth.' He was proud of Amos, and prouder still of what he had done for the little bumpkin.

He was getting a bit long in the tooth by now, and through the grapevine he had heard that Amos was talking about putting him out to stud for good, and cutting him out of the business altogether, which he figured included cutting him out of the cash flow.

His good long break in Squeezie-Anna had given him time to think things over, how Amos' had expanded the business, and how things there were legit now. He also realized that the jig was up and he had been thinking about retiring fulltime anyway. He had heard about a place that sounded appealing, out on the wide-open plains called the Great Territory of Taxless. From what he understood, life was simple there and the food was awesome, if simple. So really, there were only four things he needed: a simple life with simple food in an awesome place, and money.

He pondered the money situation over and knew he would need to put the squeeze on Amos to get some out of him, a nice fat retirement package. He decided to place a video call to him and sing him a little song by The Giggles he liked about getting rid of someone you love, called Already Gone. A song he thought would convey his thoughts more precisely than, well, his own thoughts could. He laughed to himself, 'Ya cain't make this shit up, ha ha.'

So, when Amos picked up the call, Theo started.

> ♫ Ye's a nerd if yer still thinkin ye ain't gonna pay
> Talkin bout layin me away out by meself
> Don't dispel me ya crazy fool, cause here's a head-
> line or two

And sure as shootin ye'll be blue
When those grits ye'll just be munchin with no one
else ♫

♫ So, Iiiiii…iiiiis…nearly done
But ye woooooooon't… give me the gong
Give me my caaaaaash…and I'll move along
Or I'll sue, sue-sue-sue, you-you-you ♫

Amos said, 'Well, Theo, iffin yer talkin bout retirement, yep, ya sure done worked hard fer a long time. But what news ya got fer me?'

Theo spelled it out, 'Here it be, Amos Dopolis. Far as I'm concerned, I already is done gone, and I mean right outta these here parts, so listen real close-like cause I is only gonna tell ya this once. All that schoolin I got into yer head fer ya paid off, didn't it, ya bean-pole. And like I fo'ever did say, ya kin only get by on yer old Pappy's money fer so long. You're a nice boy now but in the end o it all, ya don't get no money fer nothin, so now it's time fer me, myself, and I to get a piece of my pie.'

'Whatcha mean, Pappy, yo pie? I worked hard fer the money, so just keep yer hands offa my stack.'

Theo said, 'Ya needs to be thinkin that the onlyest reason ye got yer stack wuz cause o my stack, squirrely son. And I got meself designs on retirin to a place out west in the Great Territory of Taxless, so I'll be needin a heapin helpin of that cash y'all got squirrelied away.'

'Well, Pappy-poo, bein a Junior Advisor like ye is, ye ain't got much comin to ya. But listen up, I'm figurin ye might deserve a bitty-bit o compensation fer all ye did done fer me. Mayhaps I'll see what I kin do fer ya and I'll give ye a call bout it.'

'*Junior Advisor*? What in Satan's hell hole is ye talkin about, boy?'

'Well,' Amos shot back, 'I guess it's hard to remember stuff when yer three sheets to the wind. Iffin ya check yer documents ye'll know what I'm sayin.'

Theo took a minute to respond. 'Seems to me ye's learned

some crafty lessons from that evil brother ya had over the years. I knew I shoulda got rid o him earl...uh, uh, well RIP Abe is all I got to say about that. But anywho, Amos, ye best be callin me like ya said, and the soonerest the better. Ya hearin me, shadey-son?'

'Ye kin bet yer britches I will, Daddy-*doo-doo*.'

Amos had begun to get bolder and more confident in his business dealings. One thing he learned from his accounting classes was that you don't pay a bill until it's due, so he decided to hold a tight line with his father. He gave him a modest pay-out and put him on a rather miserly monthly pension, miserly as far as Theo was concerned, anyway.

***

The band Allbliss had formed was getting more regular gigs now that he had The Towering Trumpets brand promoting him, even some in the neighboring territories of Sweet Caroline and Ark-I-Saw. Allbliss was in his glory. Although he loved the trumpet and had the weight of the Towering Trumpets label behind him, he wasn't convinced that the instrument was a good fit for his jug band. In a bold move, thinking he needed to dance with The Brand that brung him, he ditched the jug act, added the trumpet along with an electric guitar, bass, and drums, with him clutching an acoustic guitar, but primarily focusing on the vocals, knee-knocking, and hip-swiveling.

He found Amos lounging on the deck and said, 'I think I have the complete package now, Amos, and all I need to do is write that catchy tune to put me over the top.'

Amos said, 'All that there gyratin around is gonna create a big ole stir, Ali-B. The new band might just do the trick. What kinda song are ya workin on?'

'I got in mind something about sending a love letter to my baby, one that keeps coming back stamped "Return to Sender". You know, songs about broken love always seem to work on those pretty girls.'

'Yes, yes, they diddley-do. We kin produce it in our studio

right here when ya got it ready.'

'What would Theo think about me doing that, Amos? He always seemed to have a bit of a suspicious mind about me after I drove that hard bargain with him about our schooling.'

'Pappy is out o the picture now, Ali-B. He done took a payout and skedaddled out west somewheres. He said he had some kinda callin, or hankerin leastwise, to find sweet spot out in that thar wild country.'

'That's the funniest thing, Amos. I heard he was talking lately about a place called Taxless. Is that where he was headed for?'

'Yep, that is the place. He called it Maaco, in the Great Territory of Taxless.'

'Huh, wonder what in tarnation he is going to do out there?' Allbliss asked.

'I dunno, but he'll probly do what he did done here-a-bouts. Cause more trouble than a porcupine at a balloon parade.'

Chapter 17 – Resurrection

After several years, Amos, living well within his means in a somewhat modest country estate, was out on the rear verandah enjoying a slice of chocolate pie and a cherry coke while thinking about his increasingly vast empire. He noticed some movement in one of the Tulip poplar trees nearby and, low and behold, an opossum swung down to hang from its tail on a low branch. He became intrigued, and then more so when the opossum chattered to him, 'Hey brother, how's she hangin?'

Bits of pie filling and pastry sputtered from Amos' mouth, and he began to twitch, not believing what he had heard, or thought he heard. He considered going to get his gun, but before he had time to move, it spoke again, 'Member that time we got those two giggly girls out in the cabbage patch? Never did figure out which smelt worser, the girls or the skunk cabbage we wuz a lyin in, hehehehe!'

Amos jumped up, 'What in tarnation is goin on herebout this place. Git outta here ya crazy coot!'

The opossum swung back and forth on the branch and said, 'Amos, brother, don't ye recognize me? I'm yo big brother, Abe. Want me to recollect ya more stories bout when we wuz younger, and I wuz alive as a regular human bein?'

Amos was hard pressed on what to say, so the opossum carried on, 'I'm telling ye, Amos, I is yer brother who done got reincarnated, and I kin make it a proven fact, one ain't no disputin.' He made a series of high-pitched chattering sounds towards the woods, and what appeared to be sixteen vestal virgins slowly floated into the clearing, all dressed in flowing gowns of the palest shade of white.

Amos was stunned as the girls approached and began to fondle the opossum, who was keeping an eye on Amos. 'Ya satisfied now, baby brother. It's me, it's me! Let the bells ring out and the banners fly! Feast yer eyes on me, cause I'm here, I'm here!'

He eyed the opossum suspiciously and said, 'Plenty o guys kin do that, ya rascally varmint. Git yer scruffy hide outta me yard. But ye kin leave the girls behind, iffin ya don't mind.'

The opossum said, 'I kin prove it to ya even moresoever. Remember this little ditty I penned, sumpin I sorta stole offa that great piano player with the crazy outfits and big glasses, Meltin Fawn? I like to call it "Man Ye'll".'

♫ Man ye'll be flying to heights, you're not lame
You will lead the reds, that's right, feeding your
growing fame
Your clan will poke Carmie and…make her cry
Aww, you'll be our channel, just wear a crown with
your disguise ♫

Amos looked at the opossum in awe and said, 'Only one person would know that silly song what was written. Where'd ye ever come up with nutty lyrics like them?'

'Don'tcha remember, Amos? After I got struck by lightning that spooky night them words just came to me in a flash. It felt like some kinda premonition.'

Amos gathered his wits about him and said, 'Yeah, yeah, right. I remember that. Oh, BTW, I like the brunette over there you brought along. The one with the big bottom and spikey hair.'

The opossum said, 'Now yer talkin, little nibbler.' He looked at the girl and gave her a wink, 'Get yerself on over and interduce yerself to me little brother, sweet child. He ain't like me,' and he winked again, 'he don't bite.'

***

The next morning after a long night of merriment, the opossum, while chewing on the carcass of a chickadee, looked at Amos, 'Ya know, while you been coolin, brother, I been droolin, and I mean way deep down inbetwixt.'

Amos was having his breakfast of grits and hog jowls, and asked, 'Whatcha talkin bout, ya crazy ole opossum?'

'I been eatin just the worst o it all fer the past five years. Ye name it and I been eatin it, snakes, birds, mice. What I'm tellin ya is I most desperately need a change o diet. You so happen to have some dog food or sumpin? Mayhaps even some raw eggs. Gotta keep me calcium levels up, ya know.'

'I don't got no dog food, opossum, but I got some eggs over yonder in the coolerator.'

'Well, bless yer kind soul, brother. And listen, call me Abe, just like in the olden days, okay?'

'Sure, sure, Abe. I'll do that iffin it'll make ya happy. But tell me, whatcha been doin all the while I ain't seen ya?'

'Not nearly so much as yerself, dear brother, by the looks o ya. Seems like ya spent some time on yer appealability. How'd ya get yer eyes ungoogled and yer tongue untwisted, and is that a wig yer wearin?'

'It ain't a wig, Abe. Iffin ya got enough cash, doctors kin fix just bout anythin these days.'

'Well, that's just supercalifrag…oh, I could never get that word out proper-like, but ye knows what I mean, that's great! Say, Amos, by the way, is that knee-knockin Allbliss character still nosin round these parts?'

'Yep, but ye kin just call me Amos.'

'Right, right, will diddley-do, brother. But tell me, what else ya been doin. I see ya got yerself all set up right fine down here in the holler. Managed to put some weight on those scrawny bones, too, I see.'

Amos said, 'I done took the business over from Pappy and I'm franchisin stores all o'er the southern territories.'

'Well, I'll be tellin ya, Amos a-gettin-famous, it seems to me that you be on the cuspid o makin the big time. Seein that yer so handsome, and now that I'm back, we gotta spread a whole lotta love round these parts and catapult yerself off to stardom. And you know me, that's sumpin I kin help ya with.'

'What ye talkin bout, Abe? I is doin just fine and dandy the way things is.'

'*Oh, Amos*, ye is just gettin started, boy! You been puttin all the pieces together and ya just don't know it. There always be a next level, and I got a feelin yer ready to climb those stairs up to the top o the high divin board. Remember what ye said to me afore, that you wanted to show em all who was who?'

'Yeah, I do remember that,' Amos said, 'and I already did show em. Lookit what I got goin on here,' he said as he spread his arms out wide.

Abe looked around and nodded. 'Yer right, Amos. Ye sure nough showed em ya could snatch up this little hovel down in the holler,' and he laughed, 'no differnt than all o them that was tauntin ya did.'

Amos took offence to Abe's comment and spit out, 'Now hold yer horses there ya nasty varmit. I done pretty good fer meself. Everybody sees me on all the social media and knows I is successful.'

'Amos, I telled ya when we wuz youngins – stick with me and I'll help ya out every which way I can. I is just thinkin yer a big fish in a small pond down here in the south, and ye got more in ya than this!'

'Ya really think so, Abe? What ya got swirlin round in yer screwy peanut?'

'I'z not xactly sure, little googler, but I just cain't fight the feelin that sumpin big is comin up fer yerself. And I have a funny feeling it has something to do with that silly song I sung fer ya yesterday.'

'Well, Abe, when ya put it that way, mayhaps I should think more about the future. Ali-B's idea about franchisin sure worked out right fine. When ya figure out what the next move should be, let me know and I'll take it under advisement.'

'Okee-dokie, Amos. Let's leave that ahind us fer now and I'll scurry on over fer some o those thar eggs. And by the way, what be Allbliss feastin on these days?'

Chapter 18 – Thank You, Thank You Very Much

Thinking back to the good old days, Abe had to be careful. He remembered what Allbliss' favorite meal was, how could he not. Polk salad and possum stew were a regular feature at the dinner table back then, and Allbliss never failed to visit to enjoy a heaping helping. Yes, Abe would have to be careful indeed. He thought he'd have to figure out what made Allbliss tick and get a turn on him, hold him to ransom in some way or other. One thing he knew for sure, he wasn't going to be the victim of another incident like that one with the tiger and end up being eaten again, least of all not by Allbliss.

It didn't take Abe long to see what drove Allbliss, with that guitar slung around his neck and his knees and hips swiveling about like a whirling dervish. He noted, with no small degree of admiration, that the boy had the looks, and he had the moves, too. The girls took a shine to his act and were forever dripping off him. But he was missing one thing, he just hadn't found the sweet lullaby they were hoping for.

He thought he might have found an angle to win Allbliss over, so he said to him, 'Hey-ho, All-blissy-bliss. I knowed every song what's e'er been sung. Mayhaps I kin help ya out with that tune you been toilin so hard day and night to come up with.'

By now, Allbliss had accepted that the gnarly opossum was the reincarnated Abe, but still had a difficult time talking to him without either bursting out laughing or licking his lips. The little critter had the funniest falsetto voice when he talked, and he was fattened up just perfect, too. He was the kind of character that could have played well on the stage, or, better yet, on a late-night dinner plate.

Allbliss said, 'You really think so, Abe? I'd be forever in your debt if you could conjure up a hit tune for me.'

'Yes, yes ya would, wouldn't ya, ya little knee-knocker, and ye best recollect that fact in case some other notion comes into that hairy noggin o yers.'

Allbliss looked down and shuffled his feet, knowing full well what Abe was referring to. 'Well, Abe, have no fear of me. I just want my first hit tune, and if you can get it for me, I promise to get my grits out at my favorite restaurant, Alice's, from now on until way past forever. Her place is just down the street a piece. You know that place?'

'Oh, I know it well, sweet-swiveler. Y'all kin get almost anything ya desire down there, so I hear told.'

Wanting to create some breathing room and give himself a little time to work on his plans for Amos, Abe said to Allbliss, 'Might take me a while to get that thar song worked out in me noggin, so ye just keep holdin those britches from fallin down and I'll come up with sumpin fer ya.'

As he was looking at Abe, Allbliss began to lick his lips, then thought better of it. 'Well, okay Abe. And thank you, thank you very much.'

Abe said, 'I think you got sumpin right there, ya corkscrewin child.'

'What do you mean, Abe?' Allbliss asked.

'Ya be needin to use that line when yer thankin yer adorin fans fer all their applause. The way it rolls offa yer tongue be a wonderous thing indeed, kissy-Bliss.'

'You really think so, Abe? I'll have to practice that line. Let me comb my hair first and I'll try it again.'

Abe suggested, 'Go try it out on those worshipin girls you always got hangin offa ya. I got too many idears bouncing around in me cranial sac to listen to ya now.'

'You have some songs bopping around in there you're thinking about, Abe?'

'I sure nough do, Mister Bliss.'

'Give me a hint, Abe.' Allbliss winked at him and grinned, 'I need something to whet my appetite, so to speak.'

Abe got nervous and started jittering around, squeaking and chattering. 'Here's a little thingy I been workin on, haven't quite got the words xactly where I want em though. I lifted the melody from a tune I heard afore called "It's Now or Never".'

♫ Not on the menu
　 Nor on your plate
　 Possums ain't for dining
　 I'm tellin ya straight ♫

♫ Next day coming
　 I won't be ate
　 For now eat crawdads
　 I'll pen yer tune posthaaaaste ♫

Allbliss eyed Abe suspiciously, 'Sounds like you're trying to send me a message rather than get the girls all hepped up, Abe. Don't get me wrong, I like the melody enough, but you need to come up with better lyrics than that.'

'I'm a tryin, All-beautiful-Blissy. It's just that I got so much happenin right now that I feel like a cat in a room full of rockin chairs.'

Allbliss rubbed his stomach and licked his lips. 'I suggest you get your priorities straight, Abe. Dinner time is coming, and this is Alice's day off.'

Abe quickly swung up into a tree and managed to squeak out. 'I will, I will, All-handsomeness. Give me a few days, that's all I'm askin.'

'Um, well, I'll give you that, Abe, but no more.' Allbliss rubbed his stomach again as he left to go practice his "Thank you, thank you very much" line.

Chapter 19 – Revelations

Looking around at Amos' living circumstances, Abe began to wonder why he was living such a Spartan life. The little hovel he was living in down in the holler seemed to be seriously below what he could afford, so he asked him, 'Why ye be livin down here in this rundown ramshackle house when ye kin be livin high and mighty in one o them new gated communities. Ye got all the money pourin in now and ya gotta think bout yer image, seein as yer getting so famous.'

Amos considered the point and said, 'There be lots o cash comin in, that's fer sure Abe, but there be lots goin out, too.'

Having had a long history of watching whose pockets the money was going into, Abe asked, 'You ever looked at where it's goin, Amos? Ya got all that schoolin into yer noggin, so ya should be able to cypher out how to cut some expenses so ya kin live proper-like. Ye know, get away from all these bugs and critters herebouts.'

'Mayhaps I'll do that, Abe. And at the same time see if my bean counters ain't playin fast and loose with me money.'

The next day Amos took Abe with him to look at the accounts to see what was going on. The money was pouring in faster than a canoe with its trap-door open, and it was sailing out faster than a fart in a windstorm. While reviewing the books, Abe noticed something he thought was odd - there was only one set.

He watched Amos scratching his head as he was flipping from page to page, and asked, 'Hey Amos, where's yer other set o books, the ones with the real numbers?'

'These is the onlyest books what be here, Abe. I don't got no others,' Amos said.

'Well, I'll be a monkey's uncle! Where in the name o Sam Hill is all the money goin?'

During his review of the accounts, Amos could see that they were kept in detail. The outflow of cash wasn't due to the high life that he was living, because, if anything, he was living a rather modest lifestyle. And it wasn't Allbliss sucking money out of the accounts. He just had a two-bit band making enough to break-even on his touring schedule, with a little bit of income from the business for promoting the brand.

On closer inspection, Amos found the reports he needed. Taxes, taxes, and more taxes. Payments to Social Security, payments to Payroll Tax, payments to Unemployment Insurance, payments to Territory Tax. And the biggest one of all, by a country mile, payments to The Great Union of Territories.

'Well, this just won't do,' he thought. Amos knew that when Theo owned the business, public policy, basically, was every man for himself. There was no protection for the slackers, the lay-abouts, the ones who didn't have the gumption to get off their prodigious posteriors and get to work. The general outlook was, 'If you had kids you couldn't afford - too bad for you. Maybe next time you'll make a better decision.'

Abe could see Amos' frustration and felt he had some valuable information that might help Amos out, but he decided to sit on it for the time being. He had heard from the other opossums while swinging through the trees about the growing dissatisfaction locally about the tax situation. The opossums had heard that people were in an uproar and wanted freedom from the oppressive tax system they were forced to endure. Trapped by a regime that was tax, tax, tax, and spend, spend, spend, no one would listen to their grievances, let alone do anything about it. The northeastern territories, being the largest and wealthiest of all and controlled by leftist radicals, had implemented a socialist agenda which put financial pressure on the territories and local governments.

The southern territories were divided in their support for the social programs. Unrest was stirring and Abe wanted to capitalize on the situation to, ostensibly, return society to the old ways where everybody was responsible for their own lot in life but, in reality, to simply maximize profits for the business.

Never one to miss a chance to help Amos out, Abe identified what he thought was an opportunity. He was aware that Amos was now a tower of power as the face of Towering Trumpets and was well positioned to influence the electorate. With an election in the offing, Abe crafted his message and approached Amos, 'I got me some girls comin over this evenin, awesome Amos.'

'We gonna have us a hootenanny, Abe? Mayhaps Ali-B kin play us some tunes.'

'No, not tonight, sweet bumpkins. He done got a gig o'er in the Great Territory o Alibaba.'

'Aw, dang. He'd like to be here, no doubtin that fact,' Amos said.

'Yeah, well, we got some talkin to do anywho, ye and me, so it be just as well he ain't here toonite.'

During dinner, before the girls arrived, Amos and Abe were enjoying their polk salad and crawdads-on-a-stick. 'Ya know, Amos, I been cypherin on the books lately and I got a mind to say we is gettin skewered, sumpin like that thar crawdad yer eatin just got done to itself.'

'Whatcha yackin bout now, Abe?' Amos asked.

'Sonny-bubbles, those northern territories got us by the short and curlies. That gang o thieves be suckin the taxes out o everybody left, right, and inbetwixt, and they all be in a big ole stew bout it. The election for Governor here in Tango Sea is cummin up, and I been ponderin that ye should be throwin yer MAGA hat in the ring. Somebody needs to be fightin fer our rights down here in the south. And yer the one who knows how to sweet talk Carmalita into givin us some relief from all that cash they be suckin out o us.'

'I'm none too happy bout the taxes either, Abe. And I'd be more than willin to try and set things to rights. All them bullyin name-callers from me high school days would surely sit up and take notice o me then if I did that, wouldn't they!'

'They certainmost would, and I think ya should run, little nipsy. Yer a sharp dressed man, and what with that silky mane you conjured up and those cheap sunglasses, I do rightly believe the voters will suck you up like sweet molasses.'

'Oh yeah?'

'Oh yeah!'

Amos pondered it over for a minute and said, 'Well, I'd need some help with all that stuff. Ya know, I wouldn't know where to start, Abey-doo.'

'Well, listen to me good, Amos. Yer all fixed up with the money rollin in now. So, I done wrote ye a song that fits yer style perfect, ye with yer clean shirts and new shoes. Mayhaps it'll help yer campaign and git all yer adorin crowds fired up. I nicked the melody from EA-ZY Pop and I'm still workin on the lyrics, but here be how it goes so far.'

> ♫ Dancing girls…with hair-doo's
> Tell them all to go get some new shoes
> It helps recruit…muscly guys
> Yer gonna need to help you really fly high ♫

> ♫ Your foe will be a cussin more'en any other man
> Cause the voters are always fallin fer that kind of
> sham ♫

Amos said, 'Yer right, Abe, ya need to fill them lyrics out, but it be a good start.'

'I know, Amos, I'll be workin on that. But I also know this. Sexy girls and some strong-arm men is what it takes to win things these days. A bit o fluff and a bit o fightin make fer endless mayhem and drama, leastwise enough to keep the voter's attention offa the real issues. Well, so long as they hate what ye hate, meanin taxes. So, don't worry, famous Amos. I'll be helpin ya all along the way. I say keep it simple, and every which way round we'll rope in the type o folks who like to emulate their handsome leader.'

It didn't take long before she was being courted by the party bosses, the ones who either pulled the strings, or the rug out from under you. Carmalita, concerned about the muck and mire of politics in the big leagues, turned to Mobie, 'Do you think we should do it, Mobie? I mean, should I run for President?'

'I think the time is right, sweet Carmie. Everybody's rooting for you, and you have a mighty fine agenda.'

'Yes, I know. I'm just a bit worried about the future, though.'

'What do you mean, baby?' Mobie asked.

'Well, there's three things, really. The first is about some of the things going on down in the southern territories. They seem to be moving back to their roots.'

'Yes, I've noticed that,' Mobie said.

'Yeah, they're griping about taxes and too much federal money being spent on helping people who are struggling. It seems they want to go back to the *"every man for himself"* days. But what concerns me even more are their cultural issues. They seem to be upset that they're losing their heritage. You know, all their old symbols are being mothballed in museums.'

Mobie said, 'Right, stuff like that causes nothing but trouble. But you're the one who can set things to rights. You've always been the one who could bring people together.'

'Well, those issues are tougher than any others, but I never backed away from a challenge yet, and I guess I shouldn't on this one, either.'

'That's right, Mamalita. I say go for it. But you said there were three things you were concerned about. What's the other one?'

'Well, what are *you* going to do? The food bank here needs you.'

'Oh, don't worry about that, sweetness. I've already been talking to the national leadership. They have a position for me as director of procurement, and Hillary Beendone said she has lots of time on her hands if we need someone for my position here.'

'Why you sly devil. I should have known you wouldn't be just lazing around and drifting away.' She gave him a kiss and said, 'Congratulations Mobie!'

He was proud of himself for being out in front of the situation and able to ease Carmalita's concerns. He felt a little selfish, though, when he had made the arrangements, because he was also thinking about being closer to the action, in a market with a bigger audience that he might find success in. Although Nachoville was a beacon in the recording industry, the massive market in the northeast was where the action was.

When they turned in for the night and got into bed, Mobie turned his thoughts back to Carmie's upcoming challenge and how she would be running nationally for president, able to represent everyone across all the territories. He knew it wouldn't be easy for her, or him either, but he had all the confidence in the world in her and knew she would give it her best shot. He smiled as he remembered a song he loved by a band from over in the Great Territory of Alibaba, a place known for its high rollers and big wheels. Skinny Leonard, what a great band, he thought, and he started to sing softly as he stroked Carmie's head.

> ♫ Whig ideals seek returnin
> They'll ferry yer roam on to a win
> Ringing gongs about a devout plan
> To kiss Alibaba now and then, well praise em
> Amen ♫

> ♫ Meet down in Alibaba
> It's no lie I tell ya true
> Meet down in Alibaba
> You'll be running down there, too ♫

Carmalita drifted off to the sweet sound of Mobie's voice, thinking about what an exciting campaign it would be running for the national leadership.

It had been a long road to get there, running for President. It began with helping at her community's soup kitchen and providing emotional support to the less fortunate. She had worked hard and fully deserved to get where she was, always giving, giving, and giving some more. Coming as she did from exotic immigrant parents, well, from Can-I-Duh? anyway, people continually wondered where she was actually born.

For her parents, gold digging up north in the You-Cone-Head Province was never the best option, more than one hundred years after the big rush, and her parents had known their lifestyle would not bode well for their only daughter's future.

Sneaking, as they did, across the You-Cone-Head border into The Great Territory of I'll-Ask-Ya, way up north, to give birth to her on GUT soil was treacherous at the best of times, but those days were definitely not the best of times. Border security reigned supreme back then, all the hype amplified on Reality TV shows like "Claim It or We Take It" and "Be Honest or You're Dead Meat". But they managed to pull it off and, as unlikely as it seemed, found themselves as stars on a TV docuseries, "Crab Wars", having invested their gold takings in a deep-sea trawler.

With mom and dad working the boat, Carmalita's upbringing wasn't smooth sailing, but she did alright. She learned early on the art of negotiation, dealing with the foreign buyers, and expanding their market base. She was a clever one, to be sure. Gazing out her front window from time to time, with a clear view of their prime competitor, Rasputinskia, across the expansive bay, she often wondered how she could put an end to their incursions and subsequent thievery of the valuable products her parents worked so hard to harvest.

The election went as all the pundits expected, with Carmalita muscling out big wins of the pectoral votes in the northern, eastern, and western territories. The mid-western and southern territories were a toss-up, with a couple of close wins along with some heavy losses. She had enough votes, though, to gain a significant victory.

As the first African American female president of The Great Union of Territories, Carmalita pondered how in the world she got there, the Rainbow House. It was not only that fact which astounded her. She also had majority support from both lawmaking bodies, the 435 members in the Chamber of Current Disputes and the 100 members in the Sanctuary of Old Recruits.

With their support she was able to enact laws that provided total health care for everyone, medical, psychiatric, and nutritional, along with subsidized day care and free post-secondary education.

Nearing the end of her first term in office and with her socialist agenda rolling along apace, she knew it was imperative to turn her attention to the latest security threat.

The briefing she received shocked her. An emerging character from the Great Territory of Tango Sea, bringing with him his not so insubstantial baggage, was the latest threat from the south. Carmalita couldn't put her finger on it, what enabled his unlikely rise to challenge for the territorial leadership. Nor could her vast network of advisors and security experts, other than to provide her with a rather perplexing report on his diabolical biological father, Theo Dopolis.

Carmalita could only shake her head at the Tango Sea voters' odd selection of right-wing leaders.

But it wasn't the various leaders she feared, she felt confident enough to go head-to-head with them. It was *the movement* they represented that concerned her. Being in a democratic society, she was comfortable debating the right-of-center policy makers. But it had seemed over the past few years to be one lunatic after another shooting off their mouths claiming to lead the party. But this? This was different. This new candidate could be a tricky one to handle.

If he won the territorial election, she thought, it could make things difficult.

Chapter 21 – A Very Dark Horse

The plan to have Amos elected Governor of The Great Territory of Tango Sea was a simple and well-worn strategy. With his win he would be in a position to influence Carmalita to reduce the tax burden. The rallies he arranged included very little substance, but very much rock and blues. When the word got around after the first couple of events about the exuberant energy levels and all the dancing and singing, it was rumored that as many as one-million tickets were reserved for the next rally.

He wanted something original that would blow the voters away, so he put pressure on Abe to pen a hit song for Allbliss. Abe found inspiration for the tune from an outrageous news story he had read about a prison up north, one of those liberal Shangri-La type of facilities, but just a local jailhouse really. The County Jail, in fact. Apparently, the warden had thrown a party for the forty-seven inmates, and they had been observed dancing together, of all things. It didn't take Abe long to pen the lyrics. It was a perfect song for a guy by the name of Allbliss, with his beautiful pompadour style black hair and his wiggly knees and hips.

♬ The inmates started dancin...they didn't seem too frail
Prancin round together, Lordy, it was male on male
Next thing ya know they'll be exchanging rings
Amos and the reds, they didn't like that thing ♬

♬ She'll balk
Carmie's shoddy, she'll balk
She's so shoddy, she lets them rock around the clock
She doesn't know she's gonna get defrocked ♬

♫ Amos'll take her down...and get our taxes back
He'll clamp down on the prisons...and that's a
truest fact
Ain't no way Carmie won't...be aware
Amos' bringin the reds from way down there ♫

♫ Don't talk
Hey Shoddy, don't talk
Shoddy thinks he'll listen to her talk
Ain't no way when he's the cock-o-the-walk ♫

So, his plan was a two-pronged attack. The first was Allbliss singing Abe's new song, which went to number one on the charts. Allbliss was in his glory about his rise to fame and was happy enough to throw onto his playlist the latest chartbuster by The Strolling Bones. It had a catchy melody and seemed to cast Amos as both savior and devil, in a sympathetic sense, at the same time, which of course played well to his base. Allbliss was busy practicing that one.

♫ Ye is proud see, so I'll improve your wealth
I'll begin...my stealth...with haste
I'll be lurkin in town thru all yer tears
Sellin plenty of cans and bowls of hate ♫

♫ Sneeze if ya need to
But dopes have blessed me fame, emm-emm
Cause I am hustling, too
To get you all unchained ♫

♫ So, sneeze if ya need to
But I'll cure...yer wealth...with haste
We paid our taxes to...that girl next door
And I'll get em back...vote me in today ♫

The second aspect of the campaign was to repeatedly pound the message disparaging the value of the "food for all" and "we've got your back" policies that Carmalita and the northeastern territories were promoting.

Amos' opponent never had a chance. The voters took to his off-beat persona, seeing themselves, to some degree, in him. Witnessing him at his rallies was mesmerizing, with his uniquely coiffed hair floating alluringly on a light breeze (or a strategically placed fan). It was almost like watching a fire in a pit, or a candle in the wind. He stirred up so much emotion in the crowd, going on and on about how special they were, even going so far as to call them "the chosen ones", that he came away with a resounding victory.

***

Taking over the reins of power was one thing, but Amos wondered what came next. The election had just been a series of taunts, bravado, jeers, and name-calling. No policies were put forward, at least not by Amos. His strong suit became the nicknaming, and Abe had to give him credit for that.

The intention was to reduce the tax burden imposed by the federal government. As it turned out, there was no time to start discussions on that after the election, or any other policies for that matter. The election had been so heated and divisive that the voters whose candidate had lost didn't accept the outcome. Massive protests broke out on the streets and Amos was forced to call in the Territorial Guard to curb the unrest.

He was agitated when he called in the commander of the Guards, Georgina Custard, and gave her his instructions, 'Protect all the whiskey distillers and bootleggers, cause they're feedin my base, and arrest all of the left-wing arachnids.'

Georgina asked, 'Do you mean anarchists, sir?'

Amos became more agitated and found it difficult to control his tongue movement. He bellowed out, 'The oneth creatin all o the mayhem, that'th who I'm makin referenthe to, commander!'

'Yes sir, yes sir,' she said. 'I'll lay in wait for them to start their trouble tonight and have em all rounded up by mornin time.'

'You do that, commander, and report back to me then,' he said.

The commander left and sure enough she was good to her

word. Five so-called anarchists, who were in fact just thieves robbing a local moonshiner down on Copperhead Road, were shot and killed that night. Surveying the scene at daybreak, the commander, on the satellite radio with Amos, reported, 'Sir, it appears that the thieves escaped with some yeast and copper line.'

'What?' he bellowed. 'How the heck did they skeddadle outta there without gettin nabbed?'

'Well, sir, there was a thick fog last night, and even though the Granddaddy refuses to confirm it, one of our guards coulda swore he saw them hightail it outta there in a big black Dodge.'

Incensed that anyone dare rob Granddaddy, Amos made it clear to Abe that a full-court press was the only way to curb the lawlessness. When the nation took notice of the event, it went from bad to worse. A simple killing of five "terrorists" by territorial guards down in the holler was one thing, given that the gangs and thugs looked at that as just friendly gunplay. But not so in the northeastern territories. They had gun laws and clear police protocols for things like that. If it had happened up north, they would have deployed a plethora of mental health teams, doctors, community support workers, and negotiators to resolve the conflicts.

Carmalita thought she should have a talk with that boy, things were getting nasty down there.

When Carmalita called Amos to join her for a meeting at the Rainbow House, he was hesitant to attend. But Abe assured him things would be alright, 'Look Amos, take yer Deputy Allbliss with ya. He knows just right how to loosen up those types. And I happen to be aware o how to handle that pip-squeak husband o hers, too. Those two, he and her, is absotively inseparable, and he is a music nutter as shore as I'm sittin here.'

Amos looked at him nervously. 'Alright, Abe, if you say so.'

Abe tried again to calm Amos' fears. 'Well, listen here, youngin, Allbliss can charm the pants offa them first and then you can convince her to back off on the taxes. When that's done, we kin hightail it home afore sunset. Every which way around we'll be fine, sonny-bubbles.'

The three amigos boarded the plane, but on different gates. Amos and Allbliss through Gate 16, and Abe, madder than a wet hen, in a cage through the cargo gate.

A limo met them upon their arrival at the airport and took them over to the Rainbow House. The meeting with Carmalita started out well with Mobie at her side, who was standing in awe of Allbliss, the man with the number one hit on the charts, albeit one that dissed his wife. She opened the proceedings and thought it best to take a colloquial approach, something that might help bridge the divide. 'It seems ya got lost, son,'

'But now I is found, Mamalita,' Amos responded.

'Would y'all like to sit down?' Carmalita offered.

Allbliss swiveled his hips and piped in, 'Would you like to *get down*, Carmie?'

Carmalita grinned at Allbliss and looked at Amos. 'I see ya still got that handsome lad hangin about with ya, Amos. And what's with that raggedy ole possum ya done dragged along?'

Abe responded, 'Don't be talkin bout me like I'z not even in the room, dearest Mammylita.'

Carmalita and Mobie looked in shocked silence at the opossum, not only disbelieving he could talk, but also that it sounded like Abe's voice, albeit in a higher-pitched tone. 'That surely can't be Abe. Tell me Amos, be it a truth or be it a lie?' she asked.

Mobie interrupted, 'As strange as it sounds, that's Abe's voice alright.'

Amos responded, 'That ornery opossum sure nough is me big brother. Somehow he got hisself back into the lightness from down in that terrible darkness ye'll remember so well.'

Carmalita eyed up the opossum. 'Oh, I do remember that! And leave it up to Abe to get hisself back into the land of the livin, such as it is. But I gotta say to ya, child, it's breaking our hearts what y'all are doin down there in Tango Sea.'

'We is desperate fer some relief, Mamalita,' Amos said. 'Y'all are layin a horrendous burden on me people with all the taxes you be collectin from us every month.'

'Aww, Amos, ya knows that's how we pay fer all the services to help all the folks who is strugglin.'

It infuriated Amos that the taxes were being thrown out the window that way. He began to get agitated and found it impossible to carry on a civil debate. He had sorted out the physical problem of his tongue movement, but the psychological effect of twenty odd years speaking with a lisp was not so easily erased, and he drifted back into it. 'Be that ath it may, but I be tellin ye another couple a thingth or two, Mamalita. All that rainbowin hullabaloo ain't doin ya no good. Oh, and I do know bout them taxeth, alright. And that thar ith the main problem that needth a fixin. The way I thypher it, every one of us needth to take care of our own mithfortunate thircumth… er, predicamentth. Ain't no help or aththithtance cummin from nobody round thethe partth, not in the Great Territory of Tango Thea there won't be.'

'Well, Amos, ain't nothin gonna change tax-wise. And I'll tell ya this, ya best git yerself in line down there cause ya got a heap o folks who is ready to drive y'all out. The Federales are lookin into what went on down there on Copperhead Road and they mean business. And I'm a standin with em. Ye kin count on that as a fact, son or no son o mine.'

Amos said, 'Mamalita, y'all gonna regret not helpin uth out down our way. I ain't in no pothition to tell ya what ith all a comin, but ya know thame as I do, that crazy opoththum we call Abe ith plum loco, and ya never know what he might go and do.'

'I'll take that there statement under advisement, Amos,' Carmalita said. 'What e'er plan yer a hatchin is nothin but no good, and it's sure to turn about and come back to haunt ya.'

'Listen up good, Mamalita,' Abe blurted out in his squeaky voice, 'day after day I'm gettin so confused, and I keep looking fer the lightness in this here hammerin rain. But this is a game we ain't gonna lose.' Mobie had a moment of inspiration, liking the way that line rolled off Abe's tongue, and Abe continued. 'Ye keep sayin ya want to help the folks who is hurtin, exceptin our folks what is being taxed to death.'

Allbliss had a moment of inspiration, thinking he'd lay down a lyrical red line for Carmalita. He tore himself away from the mirror and started singing the latest hit from Tom Petty.

> ♫ Hell we…don't…slack round
> Yes, we will…strut around
> We plan to brand your mates as ne'er do wells
> As we strut through town ♫
> ♫ Yes, we will…prance downtown
> May even…act like clowns
> Probably do a twirl while stealin your crown
> It'll be a…real shakedown ♫

Abe became emboldened and scratched his furry arse for dramatic effect and continued his lament, 'Ye think yer actin fair, oh, but I'll tell ya this. Seems to me ye be acting more like a Phar-aoh. Get it, hehehe. And I'll tell ya another thing. This here situbiation is a shame and is putting a whole heap o strain on our good folks, Marmalady.'

'Well,' Carmalita said, 'I just think yer wastin a whole heap o time, cause ain't nuttin gonna change with yer taxes, ya nasty rodent.'

Abe jumped into Amos' arms and moaned, 'Me noggin's a hurtin, Amos. Won't ya take me away now. We need to be gittin outta this damnable place.'

Amos said, as he turned and headed for the door, 'Yer right, little big brother. No *real* mammy would be treatin her thon tho mean-like.'

Allbliss, still reveling in the fact that he had hit every note perfectly, followed them out, oblivious to the fact that Mobie had just lifted the lyrics to what was sure to be a hit song.

Steadfast in her commitment to the greater good, Carmalita slammed the door behind them and turned to Mobie. 'I hoped we had left that slang long behind us, Mobie. It drives me around the bend to hear them speak that way.'

'I couldn't agree more, Mamalita. I sure don't like the way they speak, but I sure like the way that crazy opossum was talking. I have to get my guitar; I feel a song coming on!'

Chapter 23 - Amos Forms An Alliance

Three days later when Amos was sitting on his veranda he distracted Allbliss from the mirror he was checking his hair in. 'Hey Ali-B, what the heck is I gonna do to get out from under Carmie's thumb? I is tired of her pushin me round. Nuttin I say is gonna change her mind bout the taxes.'

'She sure is a Burmese cat kinda girl, no doubt about it, Amos. Looks to me like you need to change things up, you know, change the way she looks at you.'

'I'm not gettin yer drift, Ali-ooper.'

'Listen, Amos, you have everybody in Tango Sea looking up to you, just like you always wanted. But Carmalita's not showing you the respect you deserve because she still sees you as her son. You need to get her to look at you differently, you know. Show her you're a force to be reckoned with.'

'Yeah, good idea,' Amos said, 'but how do I do that?'

'It's easy, Alpha-Amos. Show her something she understands, *power!* Form an alliance with the other five southern territories that are in an uproar and go up against her then. Carmalita will turn into a squirmin dog when she sees what's going on down here.'

Abe overheard the conversation from up in the rafters of the veranda. Always wanting to keep on the handsome lad's good side, he said, 'That thar be the most awesomest plan I ever did hear in all me born days, Allbliss.'

'Thank you, Abe, thank you very much,' Allbliss smiled and blew him a kiss. 'I've been playing gigs all around our neighboring territories and they aren't a happy lot.'

'What is them folks like?' Amos asked. 'We need to strategize about how to get them on board with us.'

'Sure Amos, I know all about them. But first of all, though, I've got a question. Abe, when are you going to pen the next blockbuster song for me?'

'It's a cummin to me bit by bit, shifty-swiveler. Just you hold yerself tight and try not to knock them knees o yers outta joint in the meantime.'

Allbliss gave Abe a juicy look, 'Okay Abe, but I'm getting pretty jittery, so it better be soon.'

Abe thought he better give Allbliss another little teaser, like the last time, to keep him at bay. 'I say, I say, boy. Don't go gettin yer knickers in a knot. I got a start on one and here be how it goes. The melody is like that tune by Noggins and Messiah.

♫ Yer mammy done taxed us
   Now the south's got pockets with holes
  We spoke, yer mammy done taxed us
   Now the south's got pockets with holes
   The south is feelin drowned
   And it be time we rally round
   To be her foe
   We'll make her crow ♫

Allbliss liked the tune and the melody. He smiled and vowed to himself not to lick his lips, in front of Abe, anyway. 'That's got potential, Abe. Everything these days is about protest songs, and it could be a good song for Amos' rallies. You keep on that and finish it up. I need something new, and I mean soon.'

Getting impatient, Amos donned his MAGA hat in *let's get down to business* fashion, 'Tell me all bout our kinfolk round the other territories, Ali-B. If we's gonna team up with em, then I be needin to know sumpin about em all.'

'Sure Amos, sure. First off there's my favorite. Well, I think it is. Gorgeous has the most beautiful women in the world, and I can tell you that's an absolute fact. Then there's Sweet Caroline, which is rumored to have the biggest diamond in the world, and it's the birthplace of that famous singer, Neil. And Alibaba is a beautiful territory, but they say it's one of the scariest places in all the union.'

'Oh, why be that Ali-B?' Amos asked.

'Oh, folks say it's home to forty thieves, but I never had any trouble down there.'

'Tell us bout the other ones, Alibabalooby,' Abe squeeked.

'Well, then there is the historic Ark-I-Saw, which is home to the greatest boatbuilders on earth, and of course there's Mrs. Pippi, named after the fashion designer who came up with those stylish longstockings. The last, and maybe the best place, or at least the most decadent, is Squeezie-Anna, named after the all-time queen of striptease. It even has a street named after the smoothest sipping whiskey on earth.'

'I'm gonna love meetin the leaders o those territories. Those folks sound sumpin like us,' Amos said.

The three amigos hatched a plan to meet the leaders of the other territories. Abe, thinking they would need a new hook to compliment Amos' fame, wrote Allbliss another chart-topping song. Allbliss, with his charisma, his handsome looks, his gifted voice, and his show-stopping gyrations, produced yet another big hit single – True Made Blues – which became an Allbliss classic.

> ♫ Hey, they used to look funny…but not anymo
> They make me feel heady if I'm wearin em low ♫

> ♫ You're dared to…prep in these blue-jeans true
> I'll wear funny things neath
> These here true-made blues ♫

> ♫ When I'm walkin around…all around in haste
> Ya may laugh bout me…even rip off my lace
> Coo when I sing…if ya need to
> Well, hey, hey sonny, stay outta me blues ♫

> ♫ Ya won't, no…shlep bout these blue-jeans true
> I'll wear funny things with
> These here true-made blues ♫

> ♫ I might be a louse…go really far
> Wear me true-mades…right into a bar

Coo when I sing…if ya need to
Well, hey, hey sonny, stay outta me blues ♫
♫ Ain't no joke tho'…they're the coolest of blues
I'll wear funny things neath
These here true-made blues ♫
♫ Hey they're…true-true, true-made blues
And you might wear funny things neath
Yer own true-made blues ♫

***

Amos was already a renowned figure as the face of The Towering Trumpets and Governor of Tango Sea. Along with Allbliss, the two of them together were an unstoppable force, something akin to the Blues Brothers, at least for their fans. For many others, they seemed to have stepped off the set of Dumb and Dumber.

They were able to bring together the other territories, and then turned to their first task, selecting a name for their alliance. The one they selected was odd to say the least, and it worked even less well as an acronym, The Keystates of Karma and Knowledge. Regardless, everyone knew it couldn't be a more appropriate reflection of their philosophical leanings.

It didn't matter anyway, though, as it had no effect on the outcome of things nationally. No matter the amount of pressure they put on Carmalita, she refused to budge.

When he awoke at sunset from his burrow under the house, Abe thought long and hard about a new strategy to change Carmalita's mind. Well, for about half-an-hour, anyway. He remembered from when he was young how much Mamalita hated spiders, and snakes even more. He approached Amos wanting to discuss a plan with him that he thought would unquestioningly convince Carmalita to repeal the federal taxes. 'Hey little bo-brother, nothin seems to be workin to git that Mamalita turned about, and I just happen to have an idear about how we kin do that.'

'Lookit here, Abe. I hate that Carmie is taking a big bite outta our pie, but I has had enough of all this fightin. And anywho, I is sittin on top o the mountain with all herebouts lookin up to me, just like I wanted.'

Abe gave him a sarcastic look. 'Ho ho, ho, Amos, ye ain't sittin on any type o mountain! What yer sittin on don't add up to more than a hill o beans. If ye really want respect, ya gotta work hard and go all the way. And that's somethin I can help ya out with, just like always.'

'Oh, is this plan gonna work out better'n the talk we had with Carmie, Abe-a-ruinin-us?' Amos asked.

'Don't ye be makin fun o me like all the rest of the ungrateful citizenry. This plan is sure to do the trick and show her we is right serious about gettin things fixed up our way.'

Abe went on to detail the plan to Amos, who just scratched his whispy hair and said, 'That is goin pretty far, but not fer a rascally varmint like yerself it ain't. Let me think about it and I'll let ya know what to do.'

Regardless of what Amos thought, Abe was bound and determined to put the plan into action. Having previously discovered the identity of the scoundrel who had set the tiger on him, he made some discrete calls. He learned that there was an ongoing rivalry between two highly placed Rasputinskian oligarchs, Krushin Krushelniski and Gulpin Gorbupachuck (who some called, privately of course, a real nasty bitch), in a battle to prove who was the most-dastardly assassin. In a war they liked to call "The Game of Moans", it appeared to Abe, from what his inquiries had revealed, it was Gulpin's turn to make a move, so he had one of his underlings contract the job out to her.

In a fortunate turn of events for Gorbupachuck, and a very unfortunate turn for Mobie, Gulpin received a rather innocuous and succinct report on the intended victim – Height - 5'2", Weight - 110lbs.

Having close ties to Rod "The Sod" Doodirty, Gulpin licked her lips with the opportunity. Calls were made, a private flight arranged, and the reptilla squamata (documented to have previously feasted on at least three human beings) was transported from The Fill-o-Beans to Yer-Wash-Is-Done.

With her bleach-blond hair tied up in a double Rasputinskian spike, which accentuated the severity of her beak-like face, Gulpin made a connection with the flight. She had made it clear to Abe in her heavily accented English, 'He canaught be lurk-ink about vith hiss betroth-ed, I vant to be abuse-ink him all by my onlyself.'

Abe had assured her, 'Ye kin bet yer dirty laundry I'll be arranging fer things to be set just the way you need em.'

When Abe met Gulpin at the airport in a gleaming black limo, she stepped into the car and, at the site of Abe, licked her thin lips. 'I am get-ink hunkry. Vhere can I get a veast of that vamous stew I heard so much about? Vhat did they call it?'

'Oh, that would be yer rabbit stew. It be emm-emm good, Missy Gulpin.'

She eyed him suspiciously. 'That is not sound-ink like anyth-ink especial to me. Ve have rabbits in Rasputinskia. I eat those warmints all the time.'

'Well, ours be better, I kin assure ye o that fact. They be the sweetest and juiciest thumpers ya ever did sink yer beak, er, teeth into. Just head to the restaurant over by the courthouse, down on the corner where some guys are usually playin some beats. In the betwixt time, I'll be getting everything arranged on my end.'

Just before the limo dropped Abe off at his hotel, he heard her singing under her breath a song that sounded familiar, almost like a Russian version of a tune from that wildly popular kid's movie "Bartok the Magnificent".

♫ Some named her Cassock the Maleficent
The satirically, befittingly
Mal-e-ficent ♫

♫ When Gulpin dealt the party two possums, on a tray
They thought she was irrational, well, it seemed
that way ♫

♫ She is Cassock the Maleficent
The justifiably, entirely
Mal-e-ficent ♫

♫ That snake has got a rattle
She takes into every battle
When she goes on the attack
We call her C-A-S-S-o-o-O-C-K! ♫

He shivered when he heard the lyrics, thinking they didn't sound at all like the words in the original version of the song. When the limo pulled over, he was glad to be skittering away, feeling like he had saved his hind-end. The way Gulpin had eyed him up wasn't dissimilar from many a hawk he had escaped the clutches of in the past.

Gulpin made her way along to the restaurant and smiled when she heard her favorite song playing on the jukebox, Crawling King Snake by The Doors. She began to sing her own special lyrics along to the melody.

♫ He's a bawlin thing, mate

He'll see doom at ten
He's a bawlin thing, mate
He'll see doom at ten
I'll hiss and eat him late
Bet he tastes just...like an elf ♫

She grinned when she saw the special of the day, knowing the little rodent had tried to pull a fast one on her – Possum Stew with all the fixins, $9.99.

Several days later, poor Mobie, having finally just achieved a top hit song he called "My Gift Today", which some people mistook for Dobie Gray's "Drifting Away", was singing it out as he was walking home late one night from a somewhat secluded private club he had been performing at, all unawares of the chicanery that was afoot.

♫ Hey baby, hey, we are so suffu-uuused
With the love of our lives, and there's no more pain
So, it's our fame that we won't misuse
It's a darn shame, we can't all be the same ♫

♫ Wooo, send on your heat girl, then make me whole
I'm gonna sit across from your knockin soul
Yer my gift todaaaay
Wooo, send on the heat girl, then make me whole
I'm gonna sit across from your knockin soul
Yer my gift todaaaay ♫

♫ Wo, wo, wo.... In mid-lyric, he found himself snatched, gagged, and tied up, both hands and feet. What happened next shocked the nation, indeed the world, but not until the morning after when he was discovered, up to the neck in the jaws and gullet of an Indonesian reticulating python. That beautiful voice was silenced forever, but Gulpin had her comeuppance on Krushin, who could only sit back in awe and concede – 'Checkmate, comrade Gulpin.'

Carmalita could not believe the turn of events, her husband's life snuffed out in one of the most gruesome assassinations in recorded history. The first thing she did was instruct the Director of Hyperintelligence (usually referred to in those acronym obsessive circles as DOH) to investigate who was responsible for the reprehensible killing. The second thing was strike from her menu one of her and Mobie's favorite meals – Cornmeal Crusted Rattle Snake with Succotash.

DOH reported back within days. It was well known in the intelligence community that Rasputinskia had a long history of not so clandestine snake farming, primarily for harvesting their venom to use on unsuspecting dissidents and opposing diplomats. Somewhat surprisingly, even the evil state of Rasputinskia frowned upon the use of constrictors for assassinations, although the leadership had to privately admire the gall of anyone who would go that far.

Connecting the dots to who directed the hit could be a daunting and time-consuming task. That is if it had not been Abe who had threatened Carmalita. By now his previous criminal behaviour was well known at the DOH. Many of them thought it rather ironic that a critter who normally would have been the one caught in the gullet of a snake might have been the perp who did Mobie in.

Nonetheless, they still had to prove it, and that didn't turn out to be a difficult exercise. With all the metadata flying through the DOH hypercomputers, it wasn't long before the analysis revealed a connection between the three key words which were programmed into the algorithm – opossum, snake, gulp. One of the department's most brilliant agents, ID #99, had come up with the theory. She knew Krushin's MO, and knew he was currently out of action due to a nasty incident while he was training a young, super-thin, Black Racer constrictor. Being a new addition to his repertoire and not having understood that the species was not only lightning fast but also untrainable, he made the mistake of taking a piss within striking distance of the serpent and, well, you can imagine what happened next.

But Gulpin, as much as she enjoyed the poison angle, was different. She needed that extra twist in her hits, so it was a no-brainer for Agent 99. The beaky bitch was their man, er, woman.

As she poured over the transcripts, page after page of text messages, e-mails, phone calls, reams and reams of documentation all spit out of the DOH computers confirming the culprit's identity, Carmalita was dumbfounded. For the first time in her life she was at a loss, her own foster sons, or rather, son and raggedy old opossum, would go so far as to snuff out their former foster father.

She directed her staff to arrange the funeral in Mobie's hometown. Assuming they knew where he was from, she didn't bother telling them that he was born in Shatnopoopoo, Tango Sea. In what was a simple twist of fate, she ended up trapped in Mobile, Alibaba, feeling a bit blue that her staff had believed the name Mobie was short for Mobile. During the service a hard rain began to fall, and Carmalita's security detail was positioned all along the watchtowers. When her hair began blowing in the wind, she was thankful she had brought along her leopard-skin pillbox hat.

She felt that things had changed, everything seemed broken. As the funeral rites were pronounced, she began to ache, just like a woman. And as tough as she was, she broke just like a little girl.

***

Amos and Abe didn't dare attend the funeral. Instead, they sent a good friend of theirs, Dob Billin, to report back on what, if anything, he might hear at the event.

While having breakfast the next day Amos received a call from Dob about the results of the DOH investigation. What Dob told him was frightening. As he thought it over, his stomach began to turn and he started to jitter about on his chair, thinking about being arrested, thinking about being thrown in the big house, thinking about being sent out on the chain gang. And then there was the story of where the prison was. He had heard about the place before, in the Great Territory of Oh-High-Oh. Some unconfirmed anecdotes about the crops they grew and the funny stuff they smoked. And another one about a city that was gone, just disappeared off the face of the earth.

He got up from the table and began pacing the room. When Abe came in and scurried over to the refrigerator, Amos began to moan about the situation. 'Oh, no, no, no, Oh-High-Oh.' He felt they had to do something and said, 'I'm a fearin we might have to run and hide. I jutht ain't cut out fer doin time in that thar unwholethome prithon.'

'I couldn't agree more, little brother, and neither am I. I don't think we kin turn the tide on thisa one. We wuz walkin the line, and in our zest to prove all that's right, we done got ourselfs into the dark.'

'Don't be including me in yer darknethth, ye unawethome opoththum. Yer the only one that walked the line and then went o'er it.' Amos sneered at Abe and added, 'I done told ya to wait fer me to think about yer plan, which I knew was about ath smart ath bobbin fer French frieth.'

'Well, I was just tryin to help ya out, sweet brother, so cut me some slack, will ya! There ain't no need to be callin me funny names bout it. And anywho, irregardlessness o who did what to whoever, we might not be seein the sun a shinin till I cain't ever tell ya when if we don't skedaddle outta these parts, pronto.'

'*I know, I know,*' Amos yelled, 'but where we gonna head to?'

Abe said, 'Let's git ourselves out west to Taxless. Theo said everybody is free to roam about on the wide-open plains out there.'

'How we gonna get to a place like that, Abe? The law be after our hideth.'

'Listen, Amos, listen real close. I think I hear a train a comin, and I think it's comin round the bend. Let's get ourselfs over to it afore we get thrown into that friggin prison.'

They were both dejected, and it didn't lift their spirits when they heard Johnny Smash on the radio.

♫ It sounds like rain is thrummin

It's thrumming till all end

So, we won't see the brightness - never, now, nor again

We'll muck around far from heaven, just be slaggin along

Yes, that rain will be a-thrummin, won't leave us alone ♫

Amos was upset to be leaving everything behind as they ran toward the train tracks. When he realized he didn't even have time to say a proper goodbye to Allbliss, because he heard the whistle blowing, all he could do was hang his head and sigh.

Chapter 26 - A Surprising Encounter

They made it to the train on time just as it was coming around the bend. Amos hopped on, but Abe, forever the master of drama, attempted a triple summersault on the leap to get aboard. He misjudged the speed of the train and missed the grab-bar. He went tumbling down, down to the tracks below. In a split-second, three inches of his tail was gone, sliced off by the rolling wheels of the train. Amos screamed but could only watch in horror as the train rumbled along. And then he wondered what he would do now that he was on his own.

After three days, tired, sweaty, and hungry, he hopped off the train in search of food and water. He spied what looked to be some sort of community off in the distance and trudged on toward it, hoping he could find someone who would take him in.

When he came across a creek he was thankful to get a drink of water. He patted his pockets and looked in his rucksack searching for his hair pills but realized he didn't bring them with him. As he leaned over again to scoop more water into his hands he lost his balance and fell into the creek. It was such a refreshing feeling that he decided to stay there and cool off for a few minutes.

As he was enjoying floating in the water a lovely looking girl came walking along the bank of the creek. He liked the look of her and couldn't contain his excitement when he called out, 'Hi, thweet girl. I be hungry and need a place to lay me head down. Kin ya tell me where a guy could get a cot and fed?'

'No,' was all she said, but then thought about it. 'Hey, mayhaps ye kin come with me, let's go uptown.'

Amos jumped up out of the creek. 'Let me get me bag, and I'll walk alongthide ye.'

'What be yer name, mister?' she asked.

'Amoth, Amoth Motheth. What be yer name, gorgeouth girl?'

'Cremona, but most folks just call me Fanny,' she blushed.

'That thar be an odd nickname,' he said. 'How'd ye come by that moniker, anywho?'

'Oh, me auntie, Loopy Hester, settled on that when I wuz just a youngin. Said me hind end wuz so big that it fit perfect, the name that is.'

'Well, thlap me athth and call me Thally! Celebratin thuch a fine lookin behind yer whole life with a nickname like that. What a wonderouth woman, that Loopy Hethter, wonderouth indeed!'

Fanny smiled, having never been complimented for anything in her entire life, let alone for her prodigious posterior. She gave him a slippery grin and then slipped her hand into Amos', which calmed him down. He raised her arm up and did a little pirouette under it, which provoked a curious look from Fanny. He smiled to himself and decided to belt out one of Pharaohs Myth's biggest tunes.

> ♫ Well, she kinda looked askance
> When I did a little prance
> But she went hissy and couldn't stay away
> Coulda swore I seen her droolin
> And I could tell she wanted doin
> So I said, let us make some hay
> She boldly cooed ♫

> ♫ Make some hay, let's go play
> Make some hay, wadda ya say
> Make some hay, don't say nay
> Make some hay, make me bray ♫

> ♫ Just shimmy and hiss
> Sweet Miss ♫

Fanny blushed and giggled, and Amos asked her, 'Where do ye live, Fanny?'

'I live over yonder, further along the creek.' She pointed to a two-story log home off to the right.

'That looks like one very fine home. Sure is big,' Amos noted.

'Yes, it is. It used to be a group home fer disabled people in Taxless, but the territory closed all them places down when the new governor cut all the taxes that funded them.'

'Hmm, that thar is an interesting fact.'

'Yeah,' she said, 'daddy got the place fer a steal, and we been here ever since. Let's go over and see him.'

When they arrived at the house, they climbed the stairs to the veranda and went in through the front screen door. 'I'm home Pappy, you here?' Fanny called out.

Her father came out from the kitchen and had a surprised look on his face when he saw Amos. 'Hi, sweet-pea. Who ya got here with ya?'

'I found this feller abandoned down yonder in the creek. He said he was hungry and needs a place to sleep.'

Her father approached Amos, stuck out his hand, and said, 'Hi, I'm Jethro.'

Amos took his hand and introduced himself, 'I'm Amos, Amos Moses.'

'Amos Moses, is it? That sounds familiar.' Jethro studied the young man and said, 'Sure is sumpin familiar-like bout ye, boy. Cain't quite put me finger on it, but I surely will sooner before later on.'

Fanny jumped in, 'Pappy, I think Amos is probly kinda hungry. We got any leftovers in the coolerator I kin git fer him?'

'Yep, sure nough, sugar-plum. There be some possum stew in there ye kin heat up fer him.'

'Perfect, pappy,' she said. 'Let's go to the kitchen, Amos.'

Amos said to Jethro, 'Thanks fer yer kindness, Mister Jethro. Pleased to meet you.'

Jethro said, 'Don't mention it, sonny, and nice to meet you, too. Oh, and ye kin just call me Jethro, by the way.'

'Sure enough, Jethro By-the-way.'

Jethro screwed up his handsome face and thought again, 'I'm sure I know that boy.'

Fanny and Amos went into the kitchen and Amos asked her, 'Would ya have sumpin differnt asides possum stew. I'd feel bad eatin that cause me brother is an opossum.'

Fanny spun around from the fridge and giggled, 'You is a crafty devil, Amos, pullin me leg like that.'

'No, no Fanny bo-banny. I is altogether serious. It was the most bizarre thing I ever did see in all me born days. He died in the most horrifyin manner and then came back, reincarniverated into an opossum.'

'Well Amos, that thar is the craziest thing I ever done heard. How on God's green earth do you know it be him?'

'Hang on to yer haunches Fanny, and believe it or don't, but he wuz able to talk! That vexatious varmint wuz tellin me bout things we did done when we wuz little, things only he and me knew bout.'

'Well, where he be now?' she asked.

'He done fell off the train on our way over here, and I don't rightly know what happened to the poor feller.'

'Aww, that's a dang shame. Mayhaps he might find his way here sooner afore later. Let's sit ourselfs down and eat. I got some leftover crawdads and polk salad we kin chew on.'

'Emm-emm doggie. That's me favorite, fabulous Fanny.'

Fanny blushed as she motioned Amos to sit down at the table. She heated the food up and when she brought it to the table they smiled at each other. They were half-way through their meal when Jethro carried a broad smile into the room. 'Sumpin in here smells better than a corn dog at the county fair. Whatcha all eatin, Fanny?' he asked.

'Just some leftover crawdads with strawberries and custard on top, Pappy. There be some more in the pot if ya got a hankerin to have some.'

'Deed I do, sweet child, deed I do!' Jethro exclaimed.

As he loaded his plate, the food reminded Jethro of a song he liked by an artist known as the symbol ♀, and he began to sing it half under his breath.

♫ I seen the strawberry parade

A type hardly seen around here anymore

A strawberry parade

When it's hot you can see it over next to the shore

A strawberry parade

It's belooooved....it is true ♫

Jethro smiled a silly grin and sat down with them at the table. He was more interested in inspecting Amos than eating the crawdads. He eyed Amos closely and after a few minutes, he asked him, 'Who be yer mammy, Amos?'

'Don't rightly know, truth be telled, Jethro Bye-the-way.'

'Oh, sonny, just call me Jethro. But how come ye don't know who she be?'

A sad look appeared on Amos' face and a tear fell from his eye. He became emotionally overwrought and as his eyes began to wander about, he spluttered out, 'Thome woman and her hubby brung uth up, and they done told uth they couldn't find out who our parentth wuz.'

A light went on in Jethro's head, something that rarely happened. He studied Amos again, scratching his head and wondering about Amos' manner of speech, his googly eyes, and his wispy blond hair. 'Amos,' he thought, 'Amos Moses. He's that boy from the LMT Club that I dumped off at that food bank.' He knew it as sure as he knew how to drive.

'Listen up, young feller,' Jethro said. 'I knows xactly who ye mammy wuz. I picked up ye and yer squirrely brother along with yer mammy at the bus station in Camp Granada some thirty odd years ago. And let me be tellin ya, they's been some mighty odd and unusual years. But anywho, yer mammy wuz a most exceptional cello player. She done headlined the act at the LMT Club way back in those days.'

Amos wiped the tears from his eyes and asked, 'Wow, me mammy wuz in a band?'

'Yepper, young snapper, she wuz at that. Tell me, what about yer Pappy? Ye ever find out anythin bout him?'

'I done did, in actual fact. Saved his crinkly ole ass from one o his burnin stores, and then he gave me all o them years later, lock, stock, and kabittle, cause he wanted to retire out in these parts. That's why I came out here, so as I could find him.'

'Hmm,' Jethro said, 'is zat so?' What kinda stores are they, anyways?'

'Don't know iffin ya would o heard bout them round these parts. They wuz called Theodopolis's Pop-Odopolus Music World, but now they is called The Towering Trumpets.'

Jethro scratched his thick head of hair and exclaimed, 'I sure nough did hear bout them! We wuz hopin one would open round herebouts someplace. You gonna do that anytime soon?'

'Well, right now I gotta be keepin a low profile. That loco brother o mine got us in a bit o a pickle, so I won't be doin much expandin o the business anytime soon.'

Jethro asked, 'You talkin bout that evil little devil Abe?'

Amos proceeded to tell Jethro and Fanny the whole story about Abe's death and reincarnation. When Amos was finished, Jethro remarked, 'Well, ain't that the dangdest story I ever done heard. Just as well ye is rid o him, by the sounds of it, even though he be yer brother and all.'

'That may be, Jethro, but I surely do miss the little critter. If he survived the fall, he might get hisself over to Maaco and I can meet up with him there.'

'Maaco, ya say? That ain't too far from here. Anywho, ye kin bed down here till ya git yerself sorted away, Amos. Fanny can make ya up a bed.'

'Thank ye again, Jethro Bye-the-way.'

Jethro shook his head and tried to explain, 'Just Jethro will do, Amos.'

'Oh, okay Jethro Will-do.'

Jethro's brain twisted up, so he spelled it out for Amos, 'It's J-E-T-H-R-O, son. Just Jethro. No nuttin after or afore it. Got it now?'

'Yes sir, yes sir, Jethro, deed I do. Mayhaps ye can tell me more about me dear mother whilst Fanny gets the beddin fixed up.'

When Fanny left the room, Jethro regaled Amos with several stories of YoYo's rise to stardom in the local market, and even some of the shenanigans that went on at the LMT Club. But he didn't go into the details of YoYo's death, only explaining that it was a very unusual accident.

Amos thanked Jethro for the stories and said, 'Goodnight Jethro, and thanks fer puttin me up!'

When Amos entered the bedroom, Fanny was sitting on the bed with an amorous look on her face. She patted the bed and said, 'Come over here, sweet Amos, and try to get a good night's sleep.' When he sat down beside her, she pecked him on the cheek and whispered in his ear, 'Good night, snookems.'

He looked her in the eye and smiled. 'Deed I will, fun Fanny, deed I will.'

Fanny left the door ajar on her way out and he laid down on the bed. He started fidgeting around, wondering about things like destiny and love at first site. He broke out into a sweat with his hair soaked, the perspiration dribbling down into his ears. He'd never been in love before and didn't know if this was it, so it was quite overwhelming for him. It was scary, too. Being so far from home, he kept wondering over and over what he should do, should he stay, or should he go? It reminded him, naturally, of a hit song by The Crass.

> ♫ Girl, I don't know what to do
> High-tail away or stay with you
> I know you look so goll darn fine
> Yer really sumpin so divine
> Do you want me along in tow
> Please say yes, don't say no-no ♫

He began to feel more at ease, as it helped him decide what to do. He'd go after her and hope for the best.

And sure enough, they hit it off like cornbread and grits. Fanny, having up to this point in her life simply been something akin to a vestibule virgin, began to bloom. Her transformation from a sack of potatoes into passion fruit was striking. The adoration she showered upon him overwhelmed him. Abe had forever been a big supporter, but not like that! The way Amos saw it, Fanny's, well, fanny, was awesome. And not only that, it was complimented on the top side in perfect proportion. She had answered his question in spades and, naturally, one thing led to another.

***

Jethro knew what was happening. For months now he'd heard them going at it morning, noon, and night. He didn't cotton at all to their ribald playtime with no commitment from the young fella. Push eventually came to shove when the pushin and the shovin led to the bed crashing to the floor.

A couple of days later Amos entered the kitchen in the morning rubbing his eyes and he noticed Jethro eating a breakfast of fried cornmeal mush and turtle soup. He stopped in his tracks when Jethro gave him the evil eye and said, 'Amos, boy, I need to be havin a particular discussion with ya.'

'Iffin it's about the bed, I is terribly sorry, Jethro.'

'No, no, it ain't that, youngin. The way I be seein things, yer havin yerself a ton o fun up there, oh - but don't take that literally, with me sweet daughter. Now, I usually pay never-no-mind bout nobody's business, but thissy here ain't be sittin too very good in me craw.'

'Well, Jethro, you knows I just love that girl more than any other thing in this great big world, but I gotta get goin and meet me Pappy.'

'I kin see that ya love her, kid. And yer ko-rrect about that great big world o hers. I already replaced three floorboards and one structure-like beam cause o you two makin hay and merriment up thar. But I'll be tellin ya this. It ain't often ya meet someone ye want to spend the rest of yer life with, so ya otta decide what ya really want in life.'

He thought about what Jethro said while he filled a bowl with some of the cornmeal mush that was on the stove. When he sat down at the table across from Jethro he pondered the situation over as he began to eat, and then said, 'Me plan wuz ferever to get some respect and show all them bullyin types what I got in me. But I'll tell ya what, Jethro. I never been in love afore and mayhaps I'll find more happiness in life spending it with Fanny than doing *that*. How bout I propose a conjunction with sweet Fanny. I know she be the onlyest one fer me.'

Jethro said, 'Conjunction? What do ye mean by that thar, Amos?'

'Well, weddin bells will be a tollin, er, ringin, I mean.'

'That sounds like a right fine plan to me, youngster. And the soonerest the better,' Jethro said.

Amos thought, 'Sure wish I could find some of that hair medication around these parts. I'll be half bald by the time the weddin comes around.'

***

He didn't have to worry about his hair because the wedding was held lickety-split, seeing as Fanny's abdomen was approaching the size of her behind. But his eyes were beginning to wander around again. Surprisingly, to the invited guest, not a shotgun was to be seen in the chapel. Amos was excited and became overwhelmed with emotion when the Padre, never one to mince his words, began the nuptials. He took note of Amos' agitated state and said, 'Do ye, funny boy, truly take this debunked damsel as yer own? And I'm talkin bout forever till ya ain't breathin no more. Look at me, I say, look at me son when I'm talkin to ya, Amos, Amos Moses!'

'Yes thiree, Pappy Padre. I thureliest do.'

'I'll take that as a yes, young feller,' the Padre said, and continued. 'And Fanny, ye fancy the same thing I just told yer googly boy?'

'I most absatively do, yer Highness, I shorely do till the end o all forever!'

With the ceremony all nicely wrapped up, the party began. Jethro, who had never been a drinking man, found himself a fair bit tipsy and regaling the guests with stories from his younger days. Near the end of the night he tried to explain, with little success, the difficulty he had had building dams in Beaverly Hills due to the stiff competition from, of all things, real beavers.

Wanting to introduce his new bride to Theo, Amos managed to slip away early with Fanny, hightailing it off for a romantic honeymoon in Maaco, which the guidebooks had described as a mysterious reclusive resort in the Great Territory of Taxless.

Chapter 28 – The Devil Went Down To.....Taxless

Happy as clams, Amos and Fanny hit the highway and were singing along to the tunes on the radio when their VW Microbus started to cough and sputter. A great plume of smoke began pouring from the back of the bus and Amos pulled over to the side of the road. He got out and opened the hatch in the back to look at the motor. After the smoke cleared, he scratched his wispy hair.

Fanny called out to him, 'What in tarnation is goin on, googly boy?'

'Darned iffin I know, bun-muffin. Me specialitey ain't got nuttin to do with vee-hicles.'

'Well, I think I spy a place over yonder, mayhaps we kin get some help there. Let's go over thata way,' Fanny said.

'Good idear, somebody is bound to help us out o our predictablement.'

They began walking toward what looked like a compound and Amos noticed a sign on the road. Maaco – 1 Mile. As they approached it they became concerned when they saw smoke billowing up in the air.

They heard several small explosions when they got closer, and Amos noticed a hedge on fire that ran along the right side of one of the buildings. Fanny saw it too and said to him, 'Amos, I think I kin hear someone yelling from over yonder in the building by that hedge.' As she spoke, the sky opened up and a torrential rainstorm passed by, lasting only about ten minutes. The rain doused the compound and extinguished the fires, but, strangely, the hedge kept on burning.

They were soaked to the bone, but Amos began to search the site to see if anyone was there while Fanny waited outside. He saw several bodies lying on the ground, but none were moving or appeared to be alive. He heard a voice from within the rubble off to his left and when he went over he called out, 'Is anybody in there?'

He heard a person say, 'Help, help me!'

He went in further and saw a man caught under a beam, armed to the teeth. The man's face was smudged with soot, and Amos asked, 'Whatcha doin in there? Who is ya, anywho?'

The man said, 'I is what I is. Now git me the blazes outta this blazin inferno!'

Amos recognized the voice. 'Pappy, Pappy, is that you? Are ya alright? What done happened here?'

Theo realized it was Amos and said, 'Oh, Amos-a-save-us,' and then he moaned, 'I dunno. Help get me outta this here pile o rubble.'

He approached Theo and struggled to remove the impossibly heavy beam. Theo, inexplicably filled with a sense of power, encouraged him with a mesmerizing stare, and Amos felt a superhuman force enter his body. He raised the beam in an instant so Theo could crawl out from beneath it. 'I knew ya could do it, son. Give me a minute to see what condition me condition be in. I got a bit o the heebie-jeebies.'

'Whatcha mean, Pappy Dopolis?'

'Well, it musta been some kinda out o body experience, cause I coulda swore I done seen meself crawlin in as I wuz a crawlin out.'

'You is givin me the shiverin goose-pimples with talk like that thar, Pappy. Get yerself all together and we kin get on outta this horrible place.'

As they picked their way through the debris, Amos told Theo how he had become the poster-boy for the franchise with his image makeover. When they came out into the sunshine Amos introduced him to Fanny.

Theo said, 'Listen, Amos, this wuz a thrivin community till all hell broke loose. There seemed to be some kinda uprising that led to all this destruction.'

'Why wuz all that a happenin, Pappy?'

'I done gathered all these wayward folks together, all these dead ones ya see layin round herebouts, and they wuz as good as gold, leastwise till they discovered things they shouldn't otta discovered.'

'What do ya mean, Pappy, what kinda things?'

'Well, Amos, all I kin tell ya is that some folks don't cotton to a *hands-on* approach to leadership, but there ain't no needin to be goin into the details now. They conjured up some kinda ill-conceived rebellion and look what it got em.'

The wind changed direction and they could hear a song playing off in the distance, sounding like Johnny Paycheck complaining about his job again, but the lyrics weren't clear, as they were billowing and bouncing around on the breeze.

♫ Bake that mob, I love it
   They's not smirkin anymore
   Those men is now bereft of anymore seasons
   Cause they wuz wantin war ♫

♫ They's a deader lot since they started to bray
   Now they's sleepin under the floor
   Bake that mob, I love it
   They's not smirkin anymore ♫

Amos laughed at the lyrics he thought he heard and said, 'Don't look like it turned out too good fer em to me. But what is we gonna do now?'

'First off, whatcha doin round these parts, anywho, boy? Ye's a long way from home.'

He told Theo all that had happened, Abe's reincarnation, becoming governor, the conflict with Carmalita, the death of Mobie, and then his escape and meeting Fanny.

Theo eyed up Amos for a long minute, thinking about his metamorphosis from a skinny, goofy looking kid into a handsome and somewhat robust figure. 'Looks to me like ye got yerself turned into a bona fide leader, young fella.' And he thought again - someone I might make good use of again, only better than last time.

Amos said, 'Oh, I had plenty o respect back there alright until

Abe…well, I don't want to go into that fiasco right now.'

Theo squinted at him and asked, 'Yer meanin to tell me that the little weasel got hisself turned into an actual opossum?'

'He sure nough did, Pappy. It's a fact.'

'Well, I'll be a monkey's uncle!' Theo said. 'He wuz an evil one from the day he did get hisself born, and bout as useful as a soup sandwich. He never could get anythin right even if he bothered tryin. He's nuttin but trouble, that one.'

'But Pappy, if it weren't fer him I would never done discovered all the trouble Carmalita's types was causin us in Tango Sea, and all the other territories round therebouts, too.'

'Mayhaps he did, Amos. He wuz always an expert at sniffin out trouble, more than likely the one startin it, too. Look, we need to git ourselfs outta this here place and hatch a plan to set things to rights.'

He suggested they make their way a bit east to a place called Gravy Crockpot Forest and sort out what to do next. He knew there was fresh water and food there, especially his favorite dish, possum stew. They found a serviceable Ford Bronco that was parked outside the compound fence, piled what little supplies they could find in the back, and got ready to head out to the forest.

Theo jumped in the driver's seat and started up the truck. Before he put it in gear, he was pondering the situation over, absolutely determined that he wouldn't end up living like a refugee, and then heard the latest release from Tom Petty playing on the radio.

He noticed a bright light off to his left and he got out of the truck to see what it was. As he approached the light, he saw that it was a hedge that was burning, the one along the fence Amos had seen earlier. He began to tingle all over, and his muscles began to bulge. He felt a sense of awe as everything turned to brightness, the brightest white light he had ever seen. Something was happening to him inside, and he could feel a spirit entering him, transforming him. The bright light suddenly turned to black, the blackest black he had ever seen, like one of those black holes the astronomers talk about, sucking in all the light of the stars around them. The whole landscape turned black, and a face appeared in the center of the blackness, contorting into a sardonic grin. He wasn't sure, but he could have sworn it was Ozzy Osbourne.

He shuddered and the bush disappeared in a flash, skyrocketing into outer space in the blink of an eye. The light returned and he looked about in wonder, hearing Tom Petty again.

♫ Come here, come here, one God
Just picked ye for renown son
Well my oh my, just stay here
And bring over all of your companions ♫

♫ Sonny, my preference is ye, well
All around here gets the light that ye be
Well, only...ye...can...delight them, you see (just bring the tribe o'er to Taxless Sea)
Yeah, only...ye...can...delight them, you see (just bring the tribe o'er to Taxless Sea) ♫

Theo was dumbstruck, even more so than he was as he stumbled through his regular life. He knew beyond a doubt it was a message, a calling, some kind of task he had to accomplish, and he now had unlimited powers to be able to do it. He thought back to when he urged Amos to lift the beam off him in the compound. It was a feeling like that, an intervention that had come from somewhere, and he didn't much care where it came from.

And he didn't have to think much about what the task was, either. The message in the song said he needed to re-establish a community in Taxless Sea where he could make people happy. Surely, he thought, it was a "come to Lucifer moment", telling him he was supposed to "mentor" some other downtrodden folks like he had done before right here in Maaco!

He walked back to the truck and said to Amos, 'Famous Amos, ya gotta be getting yerself back there to Tango Sea. Those folks be needin a natural-born leader like yerself and be freed from their despicable oppression ye wuz tellin me bout.'

Amos became confused and agitated with the odd request and said, 'What are ya talkin bout, Pappy? Cain't ya thee I got me lovely pregnant bride here that I'm takin home with me? And I gotta fix up that trouble Abe done got me into, not to mention rethtore me reputation. There ith a whole lot o folkth back there who think I'm an idiot, or worthe, and I ain't gonna be livin like that again, like I wath in me younger dayth.'

Theo gave him a hard look and demanded, 'You listen up good, sonny.' Amos became transfixed by Theo's Svengali-like stare. 'I is the onlyest one who can carry ya off to greatness. And never forget that! I got a plan stewin in me noggin and yer gonna help me put it into action.'

Amos snapped out of his trance with a placid look on his face and said, 'I'd have to be mighty careful, Pappy. The authorities over there want to put me ass in the stirrin-pot and pin the murder of Mobie on me. But it weren't me at all, it was Abe who done it.'

'Well, son, where is that little critter Abe hidin out, anywho?'

'I don't rightly know. He fell off the train on our way out here and got squished by it. I think it only lopped off part of his tail, though. Mayhaps he is makin his way out here.'

Theo said, 'Okay, but be careful o that devil if you so happen to come across his path. Git yerself back there and gather up as many folks as you kin to bring them out thisa way. It's a promisin land out in these here parts; wide open spaces, all the land you kin see forever, and not a lick o taxes to worry yer noggin over. I knows ye kin convince em all to pull up roots and make a new start in the land o the free, Amos. In the meantime, I'll start gettin things ready over in the forest.'

'Alright, Pappy. It might take a while, but I'll give it a go. Onlyest thing is, I might be needin Ali-B to do some talkin fer me. Me lisp keeps coming back when I get nervous or upset, and I noticed that people is gettin somewhat pissed off bout it by times.'

'Well kiss my grits iffin you ain't the most perceptual child, Amos-so-famous. I think that thar is the most fabulous o idears, getting that gyro-boy to help out. He may not be the sharpest knife in the drawer, but he got the looks, alrighty. And he got a sweet way o singin and talkin to win a crowd o'er, too.'

'Yes, yes he does,' Amos said. 'He knows how to get them dancin down the street.'

'Okay, boy. I'll git ye on over to the bus station and ye git yerself back there and git that tribe o yers out here asap. I'll try to have everthin ready fer ya when y'all git back thisa way.'

When Theo dropped them off at the bus station, he stuffed some money in Amos' butt-pack for bus fare and food, and then told him, 'Meet me in Gravy Crockpot Forest. I'll be waitin fer ya there.'

'Okay, Pappy Pappadopolous. I'll come back as sure as shootin.'

Theo noticed the questioning look on Fanny's face, and how she grabbed Amos by the arm as they said goodbye to him on their way into the bus depot.

Fanny couldn't understand how life could have taken such an unexpected turn. After all, they could have just taken the bus back to her father's house. She asked Amos, 'What is we gonna do, Amos? Why don't we just go home to me Pappy's place?'

'Well, sweet-hips, I never telled ya afore, but I got me a pile o adorin crowds back where I come from in Tango Sea who be countin on meself to save em.'

'Save em from what, Amos? And asides, I thought you told Theo all those folks back there think yer an idiot.'

'Oh, mostly it's just the commie sympathizers who think that, but my base still think I'm the best thing that came along since sliced cornbread. And I'll tell ya, they is bein severely oppressed by a tyrannical tyrant from the northern territories. And like Theo been sayin, I gotta lead em out to that promisin land he got waitin fer us.'

'Are ya shore ye kin trust him, Amos? I don't know bout all them guns and explosives he had roundbouts there. And that thing he said bout a rebellion back there in the compound sounded suspicious-like to me.'

'He be me Pappy, Fanny-fairest. He set me up, in a manner o speakin, in the business, like I telled ya afore. He is what he is, fer certain, and mayhaps a bit scrappy by times, but I gotta do this thing, no differnt than we gotta roll in the hay five times a week and twice on Sunday.' He winked at her and, feeling bold, began to sing a song he liked by Knick-Knack-Patty-Whack about a girl named Sharona. Amos hoped Fanny would find him clever, changing the words around so the song was about her.

♫ Aww, you make my eatin fun, eatin fun
   Bake me another one o yer pies, Cremona
   Aww, quick git it out the oven, out the oven
   Get it in the nick o time, time Cremona ♫

♫ Don't ever let it drop or we'll need the mop, it'd be a messy slime
But I'd gladly pick it up, no - it wouldn't be declined
But why, why, why, why, why, waahoooo
But why, why, why, why, why, waahoooo
W-w-w-why Cremona
W-w-w-why Cremona ♫

She was hyperventilating by the time Amos finished the song but managed to splutter out, 'Oh-so-amorous Amos, yer givin me the vapors.' She snuggled up to him and whispered in his ear, 'There must be a barn roundbout these parts that's got a nice hayloft fer us, don't ya think?'

Amos kissed her cheek and said, 'I seen one over yonder when Theo wuz droppin us off. Let's go have some lovey-dovey time and then we kin catch the next bus outta here.'

**

After Amos and Fanny had their roll in the hay, she asked him, 'Amos, why don't we use the money yer Pappy gave ya to fix the microbus and drive it back to where ye done come from?'

He liked the idea of a fun cross-country trip and said, 'That be a darn fine idear, Fanny. We kin find a place what fixes vee-hicles and be outta here tomorra.'

They looked around and saw a man working on a tractor, so they went over and told him what had happened. The farmer asked where the microbus was, and they told him it was just a few miles down the road.

The man picked a piece of straw out of his mouth and introduced himself, 'My name's Jed.'

'Oh, hi, Jed,' Amos said. 'I be Amos, and this be me bride Fanny.'

Jed tipped his hat to them and said he'd go take a look at their vehicle. He grabbed some rope and told them to hop on his tractor with him. As Fanny climbed aboard, the tires flattened to a noticeable degree, but nonetheless they drove out at low speed to where the microbus was on the side of the road. On the drive over, Amos told Jed all that had happened, and about how they ended up where they were.

When they reached the microbus, they towed it back to the farm. Jed said he could probably fix it and invited them into the house for supper. As they approached the veranda an old bloodhound lazing on the floor raised both eyebrows when he spied Amos and then farted. Jed looked down at the dog, clicked his teeth and said, matter-of-factly, 'Got all the manners of Homer Simpson, but he's known to be one perceptive canine.' He rubbed his stubbly chin for a second, and then called out as they entered the house, 'Hey, Granny, we got company fer vittles.'

A voice from the kitchen called out, 'Whatcha sayin, Jed? Me hearin ain't what it used to be.' An ancient looking woman came out of the kitchen and said, 'Who ya got here with ya?'

'These here young newlyweds be needin some help. They's bus done broke down a ways back on the road so I said we'd feed em and I'll fix it up fer em.'

Granny said, 'Well, y'all must be as happy as gophers in soft dirt, bein newlyweds and all. I'm Granny, by the way.'

Amos offered his hand, 'I'm Amos and this is me new bride, Fanny. Nice to meet you….' Fanny elbowed him and said, 'Granny.'

Granny smiled, 'I got some vittles all ready. Come on in and sit yerselfs down at the table over yonder.'

'Thank ye, Granny. That is so kind of you,' Fanny said.

Granny made her way to the kitchen, but not before giving Fanny a full inspection from head to toe. She winked at Jed on her way out of the room and wiggled her finger for him to follow her.

When they were in the kitchen together, Granny whispered, 'That young lassie looks awful familiar to me, Jed.'

'Whatcha mean, Granny? Ye think ya seen her afore?'

'I cain't be certain, but that behind o hers sure looks like sumpin familiar to me.'

'Oh, Granny, just leave the poor girl be. We don't want to upset the sweet thing, being on her honeymoon and all. And asides, they wuz out at that cult-like place in Maaco, you know, with that guy Theo.'

Granny screwed up her face, with wrinkles rippling around like water in a lazy creek, 'I'll let it be fer sure, Jed. I don't want nuttin at all to do with the likes o that varmint. He's plum loco!'

She brought a heapin helpin of stew and turnip greens to the dining room table, and exclaimed, 'Oh, I almost forgot the most important thing! Just a minute.' She went to the kitchen and brought out a plate of fried chitlins with black strap molasses.

Before sitting down, Jed removed his raggedy hat and declared, 'Weeelll doggie, Granny, ya done outdid yerself tonight. You youngins are in fer a real treat. There ain't *nuttin* like Granny's chitlins!'

'It all looks some good, Granny,' Amos said. 'Kin I ask ya though, that ain't possum stew, is it?'

'No, no, Jed didn't catch one o those varmits today. That thar is stewed squirrel. Why, don't you like possum stew, sonny?'

'It ain't that, Granny. It's just that me brother is an opossum, and I wouldn't feel right eatin it.'

Granny's eyes bulged to bursting and all the wrinkles stretched out and disappeared like she'd just had a triple facelift. She looked at Jed, who tilted his head down while keeping an eye on her and said, 'I'll tell ya *all* bout it later, Granny.'

During dinner Granny kept looking from one of them to the other, trying to figure them out. 'Sure as shootin,' she thought, 'that girl has to be Jethro's daughter. No other child wuz ever born with a high, bulging butt like hers.' And the other thing she thought was, 'She's gonna be in real trouble sooner or later with that husband she's got, hangin round with the likes of Theo, not to mention that crazy thing bout him havin a brother who's an opossum.'

They finished up their supper and Jed offered them the hayloft to bed down in for the night. When he went to show them where it was, Amos spoke up, 'No needin to be showin us nuttin, Jed. We knows where it be.'

'How do ye know that, youngin?' Jed asked.

Fanny jumped in, 'We seen it afore when we wuz lookin round fer help, Jed.'

'Oh, then make yerselfs at home. I'm goin out to see if I kin fix that vee-hicle o yers and we'll see y'all in the mornin time.'

While Amos and Fanny were having breakfast with Jed and Granny the next morning (fatback omy-let and toast with goose-gizzard jelly), Jed told them he had fixed the bus. When they finished eating, Jed and Granny wished them well on their way.

They had a long drive ahead of them to get home but were looking forward to the trip. They had some cash, they could sleep in the microbus, and they had each other. Thinking it would be a big adventure, they headed out all a-smiling.

Fanny began to ponder the future and asked Amos, 'What's it like in them thar parts, Amos?'

'It sure is differnt than here, sweet-Fanny. They got mountains over them ways.'

'What be all the folks like? Is they friendly?' she asked.

'They is the friendliest sort o folks yer ever gonna meet, honey-bummy, er, I mean bunny. Iffin yer ever in trouble they'd give ya the shirt offa the next feller's back.'

'Hmm, zat so, double-honey-bunny? What be the food like?'

'It be more akin to Granny's cookin. Ya know, stuff like Gizzards in Possum Gravy, southern Fried Muskrat, and Coot Cobbler. Stuff like that thar.'

'That sounds good. Mayhaps we kin just stay therebouts and have a happy life runnin those record stores.'

'Well, Theo never done me no wrong, and he was purtty clear on me needin to get our folks outta thar.'

Fanny gave him a sideways glance and said, 'Oh, Amos-it's-a-shamus! Pappy's is forever tellin their sons what to do, and it ain't always the bestest thing. Especially when ya got a bride in tow with a bulging belly. And t'other thing ya gotta unnerstand is, I never done signed up fer anythin other than raisin me youngin and cuddlin with ye, iffin yer gittin me drift.'

Amos became nervous and began squirming around in his seat. He thought about the potential consequences of going against Fanny's wishes, and going against Theo's, too. 'Mayhapth I can do both, Fanny,' he said.

She slapped his arm and asked, 'What ye got swirlin around in that thing ya call a brain, Amos? Ye sure as shootin ain't gonna leave me ahind with a newborn and take a bunch o folks halfway across the territories just to satisfy Theo's *desires*.'

'I don't know what ya mean by *dethireth*, becauthe it appeared to me he had thome kinda higher purpose. But ye are me bethrothed, Fanny-mammy, and thettlin down with a baby cummin down the trackth could be a wonderouth life. When we git back I'll try to wiggle out o a little thqueeze I done got methelf into over that way, all a cauthe o Abe, and then we can put thome rootth down there.'

***

Theo's years of experience had taught him many things, and one of them was what people were saying and planning were more important than what they were doing. He figured if he knew that, he could head off any trouble that was brewing ahead of time. He was worried that Fanny was going to be a problem, just like any other woman he had occasion to hook up with, especially so since she was pregnant.

Thinking she would convince Amos to settle down in Tango Sea as soon as she had the baby, he had bugged Amos' butt-pack when he had put the money in it so he could listen in on their discussions. He was none too surprised, or happy, with what he heard. Fanny had been nattering on at Amos about establishing roots. And he could tell Amos was starting to give in to her and stray from the path he had laid out for him, preventing Amos from leading his people to the victimization, er, freedom they deserved.

As he was having his third nightcap, he thought about Amos' impending disloyalty, and it began to torment him. When he hit the sack, a song by Billy Joel seized his peanut-sized brain, a song very appropriate for his dilemma. He laughed to himself as he thought about how songwriters could write a song that seemed so perfect for someone else's predicament. He drifted off to sleep with the song playing in his mind, knowing, as only a madman could know, that what he had to do was the only thing that could be done.

♫ Just blink twixt all the tears you'll cry thru
   If you don't do what I told you
   I'z not quite as lazy like ya say
   And if it leaves ya feelin blue
   Then I'll turn another screw
   And I'll taunt ya fer all time and everydaaaay ♫
♫ So I'z gonna fight
   No more be lazy
   Aww, I'll stick you with a stick just like yer bro
   before
   I'll use my might
   I'll surely chain ye
   Next thing ya know ya might get gonged
   And ye'll take fli-iiight ♫

***

He awoke in the morning and shivered, remembering the lyrics of the song from the night before, the message they were sending him, and thinking about what was to come. He rubbed his eyes and stubbly beard and moaned when he thought about another famous song, "Another Son Bites the Dust".

Aware of the power that had been bestowed upon him when he gave Amos the power to lift the beam earlier, he tracked down an unsuspecting young lad and sent the spirit into him, sending him off to go and take Amos out. In a fit of deranged anger, he was bound and determined to have that unfaithful boy destroyed if it was the last thing he did.

Even though Theo had put *some* thought into it, the plan wasn't as devious as what he had done to Abe. Given his highly agitated state, which he was finding himself in more often the older he got, he failed to drill down into the critical details that would lead to success.

More importantly, he lost sight of the bigger picture. This was the leader of his tribe, or more accurately his next victims, who he would be destroying. You could point to several things that might have clouded his judgement, the booze, the drugs, the company he kept, but the sad fact was that he was suffering from a subdural hematoma, brought on, quite naturally, by all of the above.

Nonetheless, the poor boy he selected for the task at hand, being all of 4'11" and weighing in at a measly 98 pounds soaking wet, was sent out to do a man's job, and could never have imagined what he was in for.

***

They had travelled for a few hours, or perhaps it was only five minutes, when Fanny was getting hungry. She asked Amos to pull over to a truck stop to get some chitlins and goat tripe. They went into the restaurant to grab a quick bite to eat and sat down at the counter.

As they were eating, Fanny noted, 'Amos, yer eyes be startin to wander round in yer head agin. What be goin on, baby-boy?'

Amos explained, 'I done run out o me hair medicine and I ain't been able to find any herebouts.'

At that moment Amos noticed a young man, only a boy really, struggling to open the door to the restaurant. A man who was going out opened the door for him, and the boy went over and stood by the counter for a minute. A woman was partially blocking his view, but he spied Fanny at the other end of the counter, so he went over and sat down beside her. When he began eyeing her up, Amos' noticed the lascivious look on the boy's face. The boy started flirting with her, and Amos became agitated, twitching around on his stool. When the boy put his arm around Fanny, Amos stood up and confronted him,

'Whatcha think yer doin with me bride thar, little-thquiggler?'

The young fella stood up and noticed Amos' googly eyes, 'I'm just complimentin this lovely lady, mister. Appears to me ye cain't see proper cause o those sixteen eyes ya got wanderin around in yer oversized cranium.'

Amos took exception to the slight, but could have chosen a better response, 'Ye lithten to me and lithten good, ya thkinny little varmint. Get yer grubby thweaty pawth offa me woman er ye'll motht thurly regret it.'

The boy had to take a full minute to dry his face of Amos' spittle and then laughed, 'Hardy-har-har. Listen to what be comin out a that thar contraption ye call a mouth!'

Amos stepped over to the boy and threw a haymaker, which of course is rarely an effective tactic, and even less so if your eyes are googling around in your head. He slipped on a soggy piece of sweet potato pie as his arm came over the top and he lost his balance. When he crashed to the floor the boy was on him in an instant. Fanny rose from her stool in horror as the boy drew a knife, ready to inflict a fatal wound. She ran at him, and he looked up at her with a sense of shock and awe. Being overwhelmed by the sight of her substantial girth, sheer terror froze him to the spot.

She flattened him like a pancake in seconds flat and stayed on top of him while she tried to wrestle the knife away from him. It didn't take long, as the autopsy report showed it was a quick, albeit painful, death - Acute Pulmonary Trauma due to five fractured ribs and two punctured lungs.

The hoopla around the paramedic and police response could have filled a full season on a reality TV show. With the sirens blaring and the lights flashing, everyone in the restaurant, although somewhat put out by the interruption of their Daily Special - Gizzards Smothered in Gristle – began filming the mayhem on their iPhones. They had all seen clearly what had happened. And they were quick to get their two-cents worth in, lapping up all the drama that ensued. One of the diners, who the police identified as Roxanne, was the primary witness, and gave a detailed account of what had happened.

'I wuz just walkin near that half-moon cake on the counter goin to git my sausage in a bottle, and when I grabbed it, that young boy wuz standin so close to me, so close he wuz. So, I telled him not to stand so close to me. Next thing I done heard wuz he said somethin funny like da-boo-hoo-hoo and told me that wuz all he had to say to me. Then I heard some kinda commotion, and when I looked about, the fat one over there, the one in the skirt and high heels, yelled out, "I cain't stand losing you, Amos!" After that it wuz like every little thing she did was magic. And on a personal note, but please don't put this in your report, everything she did just turned me on. Then she flattened the little fucker, the squished perp over yonder, had him wrapped around her finger, and she asked her googly-boy if he was in any kind of pain. He told her he was, said he felt like he was the king of pain, in fact, with every breath he took. Matter o fact he said he felt sumpin like a canary in a coal mine.'

The Territorial Trooper thanked her for her
cooperation and made the required entry:
Police Report # 867-5309
Investigating Troopers: Jenny-Jenny and Sting
Incident Type: Fatality
Location: Zenyatta Mondatta Bar and Grill, Synchroni
City
Victim: Pip squeak with poor situational analysis skills
Perp: Had an uncanny resemblance to Mama Cass
Cause of Death: Asphyxiation by Crushtiation
Charges: Recommendation to join Weight Watchers
Explanation: Wifey with excellent sit-on-y'all analysis
skills employed a unique bowling-ball like maneuver
in her husband's defense
Follow-up Required: Introduce my sister to Roxanne

Status: Case Closed!

Chapter 31 - Alone Again, Naturally

They recovered from their ordeal at the restaurant and had a fine time on the ride back to Tango Sea, looking forward to settling down and raising a family. They were happily eating up a storm on the way, rocking down the highway and rocking the bus at night. On the second morning, after a particularly active night, Amos circled the bus to check the tires before heading out. He grinned when he went around the back and saw written on the dust-laden hatch – If this van's a rockin, don't bother knockin!

They had breakfast at a nearby restaurant and then climbed into the microbus and headed out, hoping to make it back to Tango Sea before dark. When they took a break at a rest-stop along the side of the road, Amos noticed an opossum over on the grass eating a small toad. It was missing half its tail, so Amos called out, 'That be you, Abe?'

The opossum looked over, dropped the toad to the ground, and skittered over to them. It jumped up into Amos' arms and started to cry, 'Amos, Amos, me dearest brother. Ye done saved me!'

Amos began to pet Abe as Fanny looked on in wonder, astonished that the opossum could talk. 'This be the brother ye done told me bout, Amos?'

'Yepper, sweet-pepper, it be him alrighty. What a most fabulous day this be!' he exclaimed.

'He shore is a cute little varmint,' Fanny observed, 'even though part o his tail is lopped off like that.'

Abe took offence, 'Who be this gargantous girlie makin bacon with me looks, Amos?'

'This be me sweet bride, Abe. I done got wedded-up no more than a few days ago. Here, I'll interduce y'all. Fanny, this be me brother Abe, an Abe, this be me betrothed, Fanny.'

Abe looked Fanny over and exclaimed, 'Well, I couldn't be happier than a snake in a rock pile. Ye always did cotton to the bigger than life type gals, Amos. And she be all o that, and then some!'

Fanny blushed and said, 'I wuz just joshin bout yer tail, Abe. I think you's the sweetest possum I ever did see.'

'Why, thank ye, Fanny,' Abe said. 'Yer a sight fer six sets o sore eyes yerself, I gotta say.'

Amos prodded them along. 'Let's git goin,' he said.

They all climbed into the bus and headed out for Tango Sea. On the way, Amos told Abe about all that had happened, well, except for the part about breaking the bed.

Abe was aghast when Amos told him about saving Theo from the burning compound in Maaco. He couldn't prove anything, but he always suspected that Theo was the one behind the incident with the tiger, given that it was clear Theo didn't like him, and of course had sent him on that fateful errand.

They made it back to Amos' estate just before dark, having been delayed several times for Fanny to fulfill "her needs" – ham hock pâté, smoked crawdads, pickled pawpaws, sow belly on-a-stick. You name it, she *had* to have it.

***

Late in the morning the next day, rested up from the long drive, Amos awoke, called Allbliss right away, and told him to come over.

Allbliss was excited to see Amos so he did a little swivel and swirl when they met. Fanny was still half asleep, her stomach working overtime to digest the previous day's intake, when Allbliss asked Amos, 'What are you going to do, Amos? The law is after you.'

'Well, the way I figure it, I'll fight the law and….I'll win.'

Abe jumped in, 'Darn tootin, Allbliss. He'll fight the law and….he'll win.'

Amos added, 'Look Ali-B, I ain't gonna be bustin stone in the blazin sunshine, nor is I gonna leave me sweet baby behind, even iffin I have to be tottin round a…six-gun.'

Abe said, 'I'm sure of it, Amos. Ye'll fight the law and....ye'll win.'

Allbliss thought about what they had said and noted, 'You know, Amos, those words got a certain ring to them. Could be a song in there somewhere.'

'Song or no song, Ali-B, I'm gonna lay it on the line fer Mamalita onlyest one more time. Iffin that woman won't relent, we is gonna hightail it outta these parts ferevertime.'

After overhearing the conversation Fanny entered the room rubbing her belly, and not liking what she had heard. She looked at Allbliss and asked suspiciously, 'Who be this sweet wigglin boy ya got with ya now, Amos?'

'Oh, Fanny, this be me bestest friend, Allbliss. Ali-B, meet me new bride, Fanny.'

She offered her hand to the handsome lad and when Allbliss kissed it, she blushed and said, 'Oh, you is a right fine gentleman, and a purtty one at that. Pleased to meet you, Allbliss.'

'Thank you, thank you very much,' he said. 'It's a pleasure to meet you too, Fanny.'

She turned to Amos and asked him, 'Ye said we wuz gonna stay put herebouts, Amos, and raise up our little youngin when he or she comes a poppin out o me. Whatcha talkin about with these conspirators, anywho?'

'Nuttin to get yer noggin all in a natter fer, Fanny. I just gonna be talkin to the president bout gettin some things here fixed up so as we kin live in peaceful harmony all-together-like.'

'Well, ye better git to it. This little palooka inside me is gonna be poppin out any day now, and I need everythin to be settled when that happens.'

'Don't worry, Fanny-mammy. I will, I will.'

And that's what he did, he got right to it. A few days later Abe set up a call with Carmalita so Amos could try to settle things down. When she came on the line Abe found himself remembering his last encounter with her. His blood began to boil and instead of handing the phone over to Amos, Abe stated his demands - reduce the taxes and take their names off the Most

Wanted List. Carmalita outright dismissed his appeals, firstly on the basis that he and Amos were wanted for assassinating her husband, and secondly on the basis that she had no intention of negotiating with an opossum. The conversation became heated, and when Carmalita threatened Abe with an opossum cull, Abe decided to play dead, which opossums are wont to do when threatened. Carmalita, hearing no response from Abe, hung up the phone.

Obviously, it didn't go as planned, but Abe and Amos did have one factor in their favor.

The Department of Homeland Security, who naturally assumed the acronym DOHS, still had a bounty on their heads as Public Enemies Number One and Two. That was all well and good, until you considered the differences between regional dialects. Given their proclivity, in the south, for dropping the last letter off many words, the department was referred to, regionally, as DOH.

When Carmalita told the director of DOHS about the call she received, she instructed her to begin an intensive search for the two rogues. Being a well-known fact that the Peter principle reigns supreme in government departments, an agent who was from the south was assigned the messaging and miscommunicated the instructions. A simple typo to the addressee meant the message, which of course was intended for DOHS, went to the DOH (the Department of Hyperintelligence), who only looked for criminal messaging and not actual criminals. DOH, being hyper-diligent at the accurate filing of reports and documentation, duly logged the request in the appropriate file – T for TRASH.

When Carmalita followed up two weeks later, she discovered that no one had been acting on her request. But by then it was too late. Abe had already made plans to force her hand.

Fully aware that Abe was trouble, just like his father, Fanny had been keeping a close eye on him and had overheard what those plans were.

The plans Abe had in the works were nothing short of absurd, so she couldn't help but bring it up to Amos. His naiveté was one of the things she loved about him, but when it crossed the line into stupidity, that's when she had to put her foot down.

'It seems to me, Amos, that you is bein twisted about by Abe and Theo,' she complained. 'If you is hellbent on bein so highly regarded, ye just better watch yerself, cause those two is gonna make ya look like a fool, one way or t'other.'

'Abe be just tryin to help, Fanny,' he said. 'He'll probably do a couple more silly things that don't work out and then we can be done with it all.'

'Ha!' Fanny laughed. 'Iffin ye think it's that simple then that's about as simple as ye is. He has got seven, count em, seven stunts he's gonna pull on Carmalita and each and every one o them is the most idiotic thing I ever done heard of.'

'Ya don't know Abe like I do, Fanny,' he said. 'He talks real big but nothin ever seems to come of it.'

'Oh, like it was with the death o yer foster father. Is that what ye's tryin to tell me?'

'Well,' Amos hung his head and said, 'ya got me there.'

'Listen Amos, if ye let him stir up a hornet's nest then somebody's gonna get stung, and that somebody is gonna be you! And what's that gonna mean for any kinda normalness in our lives, and our children's lives, too?'

'Oh Fanny, ye is makin things too complicated,' he said. 'Just leave it be and everything will be fine. We is gonna have a fine life when it's all said and done.'

Fanny shook her head and stormed out of the room. 'A fine life when it's all said and done?' she said to herself. 'That crazy opossum is gonna get you thrown in jail.'

That wasn't the only thing on her mind, though. The two little buggers she had given birth to the week before, yes, twins of all things, were a mighty handful. She couldn't fathom how she would have the support she needed for the two boys, Simian and Carbuncle. Either option didn't look good - her husband in the Big House, or her and her babies alongside Amos, and some cockamamie tribe, searching for an ungodly place of refuge with that crazy coot Theo.

'The heck with Abe,' she thought. She developed her own plan. Later that day she took a ride down to Copperhead Road and picked up a jug of moonshine for the three amigos. Amos, Allbliss, and Abe were none the wiser at five in the morning when she snuck out with the twins to catch the first bus out of town, headed west to get back to her Pappy.

The next day around mid-afternoon, Amos woke up and realized Fanny had packed up - lock, stock, and barrel - and flown the coop, kids in tow. He rubbed his eyes to be sure he was seeing things right, and then moaned and started to weep. He thought about Fanny and all of their good times, some of the bad times, and some of the sad times, too. Their field of dreams was laying ahead of them, freeing their people from oppression, and she couldn't see that these days of struggle would soon be behind them. Yes, she picked a fine time to leave him, for real.

He flopped down on the couch and put a pillow over his head when he heard Allbliss singing an old country tune by Can-he Dodge-her about another lost love.

♫ She had a deadline to eat peas and eels
   And grungy old chitlins at truck-stops fer her
   meals
   Some say it's a crime, to dine, dine, and then dine
   Sittin there in yer skirt and yer heels
   But...she had a deadline to eat peas and eels ♫

Abe was still stewing about how Carmalita had treated him, incensed that she would not take him seriously. He flew into a rage and began to unleash a series of seven afflictions on the northeastern territories. And Amos, now sunk into depression from the loss of his loved ones, and believing pretty much anything Abe told him, agreed that his plan might frighten Carmalita into freeing his people from her oppressive policies. Unfortunately, the series of events Abe had schemed up did not go quite as planned.

With the help of his most trusted voodoo mama, a transgender who went by the name of Madman Sooth out of The Great Territory of Squeezie-Anna, Abe conjured up a hurricane that was intended to devastate the northeastern territories. But, due to an unexpected early blast of cold Arctic air, the hurricane veered off at the last moment, only to come ashore in Sweet Caroline, wrecking the city of Carlostown.

Devastated about the turn of events, Abe dusted himself off and decided to cripple the power capacity of the northeastern territories by destroying the Great Granny Dam. Knowing he needed assistance, he summoned the renowned weather forecaster, Aquarial, to help plan and implement his evil deed.

The heavy rainstorm that ensued inundated the dam, as planned. However, the primary city downriver in Tango Sea, Mempistopholese, was destroyed by the ensuing flood. Allbliss, watching the absurdity of Abe's antics, came to find out that it wasn't Aquarial at all who Abe had employed to help him with his scheme. The poor smuck was, in fact, just a low-level accountant running actuarial tables at a highly unsuccessful insurance company. That's when Allbliss began to lick his lips again.

Dispensing with the incompetent weather forecaster, Abe decided to contact Hephaestus, the God of Fire (who was affectionately known as Yogi) to help him send a raging wildfire into the northeastern territories. The scorching high-pressure area that developed was pushed south by another pesky Arctic cold front and the heat wave persisted for four months, ruining all the crops in the southern territories. Allbliss, knowing full well that Yogi was well past his best before date, and couldn't start a fire if his life depended on it, began thinking about starting a fire of his own - in his barbeque.

Hoping for better results, Abe sent a series of tornadoes through the neighboring northeastern territories, which formed there but picked up steam and drifted south, wrecking most of the trees and vegetation in Nachoville, the largest city in Tango Sea.

Given that Nachoville was home to the largest population of opossums, the event left most of them dead in the streets. Allbliss' taste for the sweet little critters began to overwhelm him, and it reminded him of a song about an American pie by Gone Insane, and he began to sing and rub his belly.

♫ Say hi, hi to that opossum who lies
   Steered my belly near the jelly but it just made me
   cry
   Some bad-ass gals was makin opossum pie
   And shoutin, don't let it git on yer tie!
   Don't let it git on yer tie! ♫

Abe overheard Allbliss' terrifying song and felt he desperately needed a success. He unleashed a large congregation of alligators in the northeastern territories but, since the cold season was fully upon the area by now, they migrated south where they began killing golfers, but only the youngest boys, on all the southern golf courses.

By now, several months later, word had gotten around that Amos and Abe were in cahoots, and Allbliss voiced his concern to Amos that Abe was making him look bad. And since Carmalita was still after them, it was getting harder and harder to move undetected from one safe-house to the other. But Amos was so despondent from the loss of his wife and kids that he just didn't have it in him to confront Abe.

Fed up with the failure of the weather events and worrying about looking like an idiot, or Allbliss' supper, he decided to take a new approach. He and Madman Sooth conjured up a virus that only thrived in cold weather, and he mailed it to thousands of poor residents in the northeastern territories. The virus was supposed to put everyone in a state of rebellion, but only had the effect of increasing their love of opossum pie.

Discovering this, Abe traveled to the northeastern territories to try and save his kinfolk. While he was trying to talk to another opossum, he was captured by the police due to the Most Wanted APB. The thing that gave him away, which he never thought through, was that other opossums didn't have the capacity of speech. But he managed to escape when he sweet-chattered a female opossum into unlocking his cage, which allowed him to begin his return trip to Tango Sea. On his journey back, Abe passed over some of the biggest playgrounds he had ever seen. They were teeming with children. Children who would grow up to become adults, adult northerners who would more than likely enact, yet again, more policies that would subjugate the south.

He had a thought, or more correctly, a kernel of evil, fester in his cranial sac. Something so vile and despicable, a twisted twist on the alligator thing earlier that had wiped out so many young boys, that even he couldn't stomach the thought of it. He tried desperately to put it out of his mind and carried on his way, hoping he could resist the temptation to talk it over with Madman Sooth when he got home.

As it turned out, fortunately for both Abe and the children, Abe's memory was about as long as the short end of a sweet potato, and it never crossed his mind again.

So, Abe continued on his way, avoiding one disaster after another, almost anyway. He was slightly wounded when a hunter tried to shoot him out of a tree, lopping off his left ear. He scampered away and stopped to rest at a pond on a golf course.

Having forgotten about his previous plague, he barely escaped the jaws of an alligator, which happened to have several size-three golf shoes littered about it nearby.

He shuddered at the thought of what could have been and headed for home, hoping that Amos wasn't pissed-off with the way things had turned out, but at the same time more determined than ever to make Amos look good.

Chapter 33 – Exodus

Abe made it back to Tango Sea to find Amos sulking on the back deck about missing Fanny and the twins. Amos said to him, 'We be needin a new plan to sort out this mess we's in. You seen Ali-B anywherebouts, Abe?'

Abe grinned, 'I seen him over yonder at Alice's Restaurant havin a heapin helpin o grits and hog jowls, dear brother.'

'Well, I need to talk to him, but listen up. Things ain't xactly workin out with Carmalita, seein as she still wants to throw us in jail. And Pappy's got a right fine idear that we need to be makin tracks back out west to where he's at. It's a promisin land out that way, and he done told me we'd find our way to freedom out thar. And on top o that, I might just be able to find me sweet bride at her Pappy's place.'

'Whatcha goin on about, Amos tryin-t-tame-us. I'll set that Carmalita to rights once and fer all, and then we'll be free.'

'Mayhaps that be the way yer lookin at it, Abe, but ye ain't goin to get another chance to make me look like a fool. I have absatively had it with yer failed attempts to *set things right*.'

'Hey, Amos, don't brush me off like that. I ain't a standin in yer shadow!'

'Matter o fact ye is, ya little eight-pound furball. And I'm a tellin ya, one way or t'other, we is gonna high-tail it outta here. We's gonna venture way out west to the promisin land. Pappy's got everthin ready fer the whole tribe out there.'

'What tribe ya talkin about, Amos?' Abe asked.

'I'm talkin about all the folks who voted fer me and is fightin against those left-wing nutty-nuts.'

Abe relented on his desire to change Amos' mind, and asked, 'They got any girls out in that thar territory, Amos?'

'Similar to herebouts, far as I kin tell, mayhaps even *furrier*, if that's what yer lookin fer.'

'What is we a waitin fer, then, Amos Moses. If ye think it's the bestest plan fer us then take us to that promisin land yer talkin bout, pronto.'

Amos said, 'We be goin quicker than ya kin skin a cat.' Abe cringed, and Amos apologized, 'Oops, sorry bout that, Abeydaby.'

Amos went off to track down Allbliss and as he was winding his way down Baker Street, he started thinking about Fanny and the kids. He thought how nice it would be to be with them and maybe just renting some land in a lazy little town and forget about everything. But he realized he couldn't do that, and that deep down in his heart he was sure he had to follow Theo's calling, and there was still lots of work to be done.

His spirits lifted when he heard that sweet sounding voice he recognized so easily, Allbliss, coming from around the corner, practicing his "Thank you, thank you very much" line.

Amos called out, 'Listen close Ali-B, I be needin ya to help me gather up the tribe. We be headin fer a promisin land out in a westerly di-rection.'

'Why are we doing that, Amos?' Allbliss asked. 'I've got all my fans behind me here.'

'Pappy done told me it is the land o milk and honey, and I need ya to sweet talk all o them thar fans you talkin about, and everyone else who will hear ya, to follow along.'

'Will do, Amos, so long as I can bring my fans with me.'

'Ye sure nough can. We needs to be movin out asap, so let's start gatherin up the tribe.'

***

They were all gung-ho for the big adventure. Abe had had too many close calls over the years and didn't like the idea of Carmalita possibly throwing him in jail, or more than likely in a stewing pot. He figured, after his recent failures, it was time for him to make a new start. They gathered up the tribe with Allbliss singing and wiggling around like a fish on a hook and departed in a column, headed for the OKAY Bridge crossing over the Mrs.

Pippi River in Squeezie-Anna.

When they arrived, they found that the bridge was being patrolled by GUT Boredom Services Guards, on the lookout for Amos and a mangy opossum.

Being wise to what was up, Amos sent Allbliss on ahead to try and distract the guards. He put on the show of his life singing the full eighteen-minute version of Alice's Restaurant, which delighted the guards, and gave Amos and Abe a chance to break free from the tribe and sneak past them down along the river.

When the show was over, the guards inspected everyone in the tribe and, based on scouting reports they had received earlier, would not allow them to cross. Allbliss led the tribe, on foot, along the river to where Amos and Abe had headed for and met up with them five miles downstream.

They decided to camp for the night and learned that every bridge across the Mrs. Pippi River was blocked.

At sun-up Amos decided to march the group along the riverbank, looking for a way across, and after four hours of walking they stopped for a rest. As Amos was surveying the scene, dark clouds raced across the sky, and he was instantly struck by lightning. There was a thunderous boom overhead and Amos did a twirl and three backflips, landing directly in front of Allbliss. He spun around to face Allbliss and for a split second he swore he saw Theo's face winking at him. He blinked and then realized he was nose-to-nose with Allbliss. Amos gave him a penetrating, mesmerizing stare for a full minute and then told him to bring up the beat to "Stayin Alive" on his iPhone. Allbliss, in an otherworldly state of mind, tuned it in. Amos began to dance, with his arms and legs shooting out in all directions, not dissimilar from the manic gyrations of Elaine Benes. Allbliss, who was dumbstruck at the sight, involuntarily started to sing some lyrics which he had never heard before. As Amos was dancing, the river suddenly parted. With Amos in the lead the tribe began to cross the river, dancing behind him, their arms and legs all akimbo, while performing a disjointed version of the locomotion. Allbliss, who was three steps behind Amos, carried on singing and swiveling his hips like there was no tomorrow.

♫ See the water breakin and all the folks is quakin
They will cross the divide, cross the divide
The chosen ones are achin from all the tax she's
takin
They will cross the divide, cross the divide
Divide, divide, divide, divide, cross the divide, cross
the divide
Divide, divide, divide, divide, cross the divide, cross
the divide ♫

As the river continued to back up, the water began to spill over the riverbanks and destroyed the levees on the Squeezie-Anna side, flooding houses, drowning residents, and destroying the crops.

The Boredom Guards, who by now were in hot pursuit, were caught in the deluge as the river returned to normal and were washed away across the surrounding fields and down the river.

Thousands of Amos' followers made it across the river but, unfortunately, hundreds got stuck in the mud and muck with the guards and were drowned when the water returned to normal before they finished crossing.

Chapter 34 - The Wanderer

After the success, and failure, of crossing the Mrs. Pippi River, the tribe traveled across the territories for forty days searching for the promisin land. Even though Amos got most of his tribe across the river, he couldn't get out of his head the image of the tribe members perishing during the crossing. The responsibility he felt for it overwhelmed him and he couldn't bring himself to face the tribe, so he asked Allbliss to speak in his place.

Allbliss was worried about Amos' apparent depression, and he was also worried about the rest of the tribe, who were becoming cantankerous about the long journey. He thought they needed to make some decisions about what they should do, so he tracked down Abe to talk it over.

'Lookee here, Abe,' Allbliss said, 'we need to find that promising land and settle ourselves down.'

Abe said, 'I love wanderin round, seein all new countryside like this here in front o us, Allbliss.'

Allbliss said, 'Well, we need to establish a community somewhere, and maybe we should do that when we find the next watering hole. I noticed the tribe is getting tired and hungry.'

Abe said, 'I is just maybe the most opposite o yerself, Allbliss. I likes to play life just roamin and wanderin round. Ya know, when I fell offa that train and wuz on me own fer all that time, I just loved to wander round, swingin up and down.'

'Well, that may be, Abe, but if we start running out of snakes and gophers, you just might find yourself swimming about in a hot tub, and I mean a *really* hot tub.'

Abe began twitching about and realized that there wasn't a tree to be found on the open plain where he could escape to. Wanting to take the thought of a stewing pot out of Allbliss' mind, he started rubbing up against his ankle and said, 'Take us to that watering hole, Alibaba. Settling down somewheres might give me time to write ye another hit song.'

Allbliss laughed, 'Now you're talking my language, Abe. Let's get going.'

***

Through his vast network of spies, Theo heard that the tribe had decided to put down roots and were not going to seek him out. He was enraged with what was happening, so to punish them he kept moving the sun, moon, and north star around, leading the tribe to wander in the desert for two more months.

After yet another hot and dusty day Abe approached Amos, who had long since recovered from his depression, and said, 'Theo's just pulling yer leg, Amos. Look around yerself, there's no promisin land out here. All there be is cactus, dust, and critters we're all sick o eatin.'

Amos didn't believe Abe's claim about Theo but couldn't disagree with the rest of what he said. 'I got a hankerin on for a big ole Taxless brisket meself, too, Abe. But pappy said we gotta do this thing, and we is a gonna do it. So don't go badmouthing him again or I'll feed ya to the vultures!'

Abe hissed at Amos and then began to play dead.

Amos, pretty well fed up with Abe's endless string of failures, gave him a kick and left him for dead, and continued to lead his tribe across the plains.

Mad as a hatter but not wanting to be left behind yet again, Abe picked himself up and skittered along behind.

Chapter 35 – Revolution

Still wandering in the scorching desert, with not a hair medication store in sight, Amos was aware that the tribe was dusty, thirsty, disheartened, and in a foul mood. Sick and tired of eating skewered snake and grilled gopher, they hit the wall when they ran out of Sweet Baby Ray's Maple Bourbon barbeque sauce.

With water scarce, mothers in the tribe were wailing and children were crying day and night. At least there was very little need for diapers and toilet paper. After all, nothing going in equals nothing coming out. 'Funny how dehydration can do that to a person,' Abe thought.

The men had had enough of it all, being pestered 24/7 by their wives with an endless stream of laments and denunciations, complaining not only about their thirst, but also about the foul stench of the whole lot of them.

A rebellion began to stew in the ranks and Abe, Allbliss and a few of the leading tribe members were fearful for what might come of it. The group of grumblers approached Amos, pleading for relief from their thirst.

John, the leader of the pack, said to Amos, 'A revolution is in the air, Amos. The tribe is starting to get highly pissed-off with you, wandering around all helter skelter like this.'

'Oh, be that true, comrade? They're thinkin I'm some kinda fool, is they?' Amos asked.

John's buddy Paul spoke up, 'It's approaching that point, Amos. I told ya we done took a wrong turn at Albuquerque, but ya wouldn't listen.'

And his friend George added, 'Yeah, Amos, right after we passed the Alamo, remember?'

Blingo stepped in between them, tapped his thighs a few beats, and said, 'Don't make me shout it out, dude, you better tell us everything will be...ALRIGHT!'

The foursome then broke out into four-part harmony.

♫ Ya need to fear our constipatioooon

Hells bells…we can't go

Ye ain't been feedin us steak or ham ♫

♫ Sure hope ya make some restitutiooooon

Hells bells…let it flow

Give us water, or maybe flan ♫

♫ Hey, iffin ye don't and we got nothin to eat

Dude we say, we is gonna make you bleat ♫

♫ Note we're low and cannot see

Your light

Note we're low and cannot see (your light)

Note we're low and cannot see (your light) ♫

Amos interrupted, 'I'm wantin it to be alright, too, ya mopheads, but what the heck do y'all think I kin do bout it? Wave a magic wand herebouts and have some water appear outta nuttin?'

Abe spoke up, 'Goodness toogly-woogly, Amos. Ye kin gather up some o those cactus innards and purify em, ya know, turn em into water, cain't ya?'

Amos started getting stressed with the pressure they were putting on him and said, 'Ye keep talkin tho thilly I might jutht rub thome o thothe thar juicy yellow innardth in yer theedy little eye, ya fool.'

Another one of the tribe members broke in, 'Easy Amos, we gotta try sumpin. Mayhaps ye kin just give it a try with that funny hooked stick ye been luggin round all ferever.'

'What ye thpectin me to do, whack the cactuth and have water come a flowin out o it?'

The man pleaded, 'I'm tellin ya, Amos, ye gonna have a most disastrous rebellion on yer hands iffin ye don't do sumpin posthaste.'

'What kinda word ya thayin there, poththathte?'

'Well, how bouts lickety-split then.'

'Oh, now I knowth what ye ith talkin bout. Okay, let me give that cactuth over yonder a whack upthide the head and we'll find out what happenth.'

They went over to the cactus and Amos lined up the top of it, trying to keep his googly eyes from wandering off target. He took a mighty swing and missed completely, swinging high over the top. When he spun around he fell to the ground. Everyone looked at each other with dismay and squinted their eyes, wondering what in the world was going to become of them.

He picked himself up off the ground, dusted himself off, and lined up again for another shot at it. He figured that since he had aimed for the top the last time, he would aim lower hoping for a body shot, or at least whack some part of it. Sure enough, when he swung this time, he took the top completely off and liquid started gushing out like a broken fire hydrant.

The men began whooping and running about, gathering up buckets to capture the precious liquid. It turned out that the sour cactus juice had in fact been turned into a seemingly endless supply of fresh water, which quenched their thirst and redeemed their belief in Amos.

Now that he had everyone back in line, the women and children, although still somewhat miffed about their diet of snakes and gophers, had finally shut up.

***

They continued their trek and weeks later camped on the outskirts of a one-horse town. The next day Amos went into town and was having a café pappapoochey and gizzard crème stuffed croissant at a broken-down saloon, and in walked none other than his father-in-law, Jethro. He spotted Amos at a counter stool and sat down beside him. 'Hi Amos,' he said, 'ya finally made it back to see yer bride, eh boy!'

'Well, Jethro, Theo done told me to do some stuff out this way, and I was hopin to see me betrothed and sweet children.'

'I'll be tellin ya this, Amos. Ya need to make some time fer that wife o yers and those youngins she got there.'

Amos thought about it and nodded his head. 'I'll do xactly that, Jethro, but I gotta get me tribe out to Theo.'

'What ya gotta do, Amos, is stay clear of that dastardly dude and make time to take care of yer wifey and two youngins. I heard all about what went on with him over there in Maaco a piece back, and me daughter and grandkids don't want to be associated with any of his kind of trouble. You hear clearly what I'm tellin ya, Amos?'

'Yep, I surely do, Jethro. But he's me pappy. I been missin me lovely gal and kids sumpin terrible goin on ferever now. So, when I get the tribe over to Gravy Crockpot Forest, I'll be done with him.'

'Good, good, Amos. That's just to the north of here. Tell ya what, let's have us a feast to celebrate. I'm gonna order up a big ole mess o barbequed ham hocks and apricot gumbo soup.'

'Golllly, Jethro, that be one o me and Fanny's favorite meals.'

'I know, Amos. And we'll git the ham hocks burnt up a bit, ya know, Cajun-like.'

'Mayhaps we kin order some extra fer Fanny and the twins, too,' Amos suggested.

'Good idear. She'll be so happy to see you, Amos, but you know her, she'll be even more so iffin ya bring some extra food with ya.'

The discussion made Amos think about how much he had been missing Fanny. And a song that had repeated itself over and over in his head since she had taken off with the kids came back to haunt him. It was that smash hit by Witherin Bill "Ain't No Funtime (when she's gone)", and it replayed in his head once again.

♫ Don't have no fun time…I'm alone
   Seems so cold now…there's no hay
   Don't have no fun time…I'm aloooone
   Member pullin off yer thong
   Every time we hit the hay ♫

♫ Can we get back…and play some
   Mayhaps she still…wants to play

Don't have no fun time...I'm aloooone
That old barn was like a throne
Every time we hit the hay ♫

Amos got back to the tribe after having dinner and a fine reunion with Fanny and the children. On his way back he had thought things over, all the things he had been through, his short-lived glory and the strife that came with it. When he arrived at their encampment, he tracked down Allbliss and told him he had his family to take care of and as soon as he got the tribe over to Theo, that's what he was going to do.

Allbliss was confused and wasn't sure what was to come. 'But Amos, how am I going to get my career restarted if you do that?'

Amos assured him, 'Don't worry about a thing, Ali-B. I wouldn't cut ya loose and leave ya high-and-dry. We'll figure out sumpin fer ya.'

'Well,' Allbliss said, 'I'll have to trust you on that, Amos. But how are you going to restore your good name and prominence?'

'I'm none too sure I got it in me to bother with that, Ali-B,' he said. 'Me sweet bride and children need me.'

'But so does Carmalita,' Allbliss pointed out. 'She's not going to stop her search for you just because you say the game is over.'

'Oh, Ali-B, I'll figure that out later. Fer now I'll just find Theo and hand off all these poor folks to him.' He waved his arms around at the sea of people camped out on the plain. 'They's a sorry lot, and I've had my fill o them anywho.'

The excitement was evident on Amos' face the next morning when he said to Allbliss, 'Jethro done told me that the forest is just over yonder,' as he pointed off to the north. 'I can hand off the tribe to Theo and then get back to me bride and youngins.'

They packed up camp and headed out, and sure enough he soon spied the forest off in the distance. He elbowed Ali-B, 'Look, now's me chance fer freedom. I'll be makin tracks fer fair Fanny in no time.'

When they arrived, Theo was nowhere to be found. It was easy enough to see that, as the forest had been burned out in a freak accident involving a herd of cattle, a branding iron, and an unexpected eruption of Taxless tea from underground. Amos was beside himself with frustration, but they set up camp anyway and somehow managed to eke out a meager existence there, waiting for divine intervention, or at least for Theo to appear.

Theo knew what Amos' plan was, and he had concocted his own plan to make sure that Amos, and especially Abe, were totally beholding to him. He was going to make them suffer a little bit, but still provide for their necessities. At unexpected intervals at night, at the controls of a helicopter, he dropped food and water off to the tribe.

After two weeks, Amos decided he needed to go out and search for Theo. He found himself turned about and lost while searching to the west for deliverance, and he did find it one night, but not the kind of deliverance he was expecting. He managed to escape before sun-up, leaving the buggering buggers behind, while rubbing his behind. He sorely wanted to head back east and return to the tribe, but most of all to Fanny. Thinking he was travelling east, he ended up heading further west instead, as Theo had moved the north star to the south again to bring Amos to him.

One morning while still travelling west, Amos saw smoke signals coming from a hill, and as he approached it he began to sneeze repeatedly. As he got closer, he noticed a sign that read Mount Sinusitis, Pop. = 1, Ht. = 666Ft. He was concerned about going up the hill, thinking that at its apex he might meet Beelzebub, but something inside propelled him to climb the hill. He was seriously relieved when he encountered Theo at the top, and never really thought through his fear about meeting the devil.

When Theo saw Amos, he bellowed out, 'Amos, I'm a tellin ya, yer losin site o the goal, boy!'

Amos entered a trance, like the last time, as he gazed into Theo's eyes. 'I got some big plans fer yerself and ain't a one of em got anything to do with buildin bridges o'er yer wifey's troubled waters. First off, ye's gonna cow-tow to what I be tellin ya, and next up I is gonna bring that shifty opossum down once and fer all. Abe's been steerin ya off track in everything he's done, but I'm the one who will set ye off to greatness, like I telled ya afore. And another thing yer both gonna realize is that sooner or come lately, ye'll have to serve somebody, and that somebody is yers truely!'

Amos begged, 'Oh, Theo, I'm a pleadin with ya, give him a break. He's me brother, after all. I'll git him in line when I get back there.'

'Okay, boy, and ditch any ideas ye got about settlin down with Fanny. And stop that snarly ole opossum from doin those drugs he keeps takin. I'll have none o that funny stuff out in these parts when y'all git here.'

'I will, I will, Theo-top-Adored. I'll get back there and bring em all out here.'

'No, no!' Theo bellowed. 'Meet me back in Maaco. And hold yer horses a minute. Afore ya go, I be needin ya to take these here ten rules back to the tribe. They best know them inside and upside down afore they come out thisa way.'

'What is they, Pappy?'

'Come closer, son, and write this down,' Theo said, and he

revealed what he called the Ten Truths of Temerity. Amos inscribed them on his etch-a-sketch and got ready to return to the tribe.

Theo boomed out, 'Hold on there, youngster! That ain't the end o it. I gotta tell ya the rules round it all. Some fundamentalist words to live by, ya know.' Theo explained the rules, one after the other, which Amos found difficult to take in. He noticed Amos' eyes googling around in his head and said, 'Listen up, Amos. Ye tell everyone in the tribe I got their backs like nobody ever did afore and nobody ever will agin. I kin promise them that, and ye is the one that's a gonna help me do it.'

'Well Pappy, what else do I gotta do?'

Theo decided to go back to his all-time favorite hit by Billy Joel because it had such appropriate lyrics for almost any situation, and he belted it out for Amos in his crackly voice.

♫ Ye'll lead the right
  If ye ain't lazy
  Ye is sure the type o lispy hick
  I be needing more ♫
♫ Wear yer hero tights
  Free the confederacy
  Ya might get gonged; we'll see how it goes
  Just go out and fi-iiight ♫

'I don't rightly know what that means, Pappy. Sounds like I is gonna get into some kinda fisticuffs, and ye knows that ain't me speciality.'

Theo said, 'Don't worry bout it fer now, Amos. It'll all come clear to ya later.'

When Amos turned to go Theo grabbed him by the back of his collar and said, 'One other thing, Amos. I need ya to build me an altar to contain the Ten Truths of Temerity. Y'all kin use it as a place to give thanks to me fer savin yer sorry hides. There's a bunch of stuff I want ya to put in it, too. Here's a list I done made up, so make sure the altar is big enough to get everything in there.'

***

When Amos returned to the tribe three weeks later, he realized the etch-a-sketch had been wiped clean due to having been shaken around on his return journey, and he didn't remember what the Ten Truths were.

With his shoulders slumped, he wandered across the great plain again, searching for Theo so he could rewrite the Ten Truths. One night Abe (who had secretly followed him this time) appeared from behind a cactus. He made the mistake of jumping on top of it and yelped as he fell to the ground. He got up, shook his head, and told Amos, 'You need to be inscribin them Truths on yer iPad so ya don't mess em up agin when ye take em back to the tribe.'

'I cain't find Theo and cain't remember xactly what they was, Abe, but I remember some o what he telled me bout the rules.'

'Tell me what he said, and I'll do me best to cypher out what he meaned by it all, Amos, or therebouts close enough, leastwise fer the girls I go round with.'

When Amos described what Theo had told him, Abe translated their meaning, and Amos inscribed them on his iPad:

1. Do it to him afore he does it to you

2. If ya want to run with the dog yer gonna have to bite a few folks

3. Pick a laywer ya kin turn the screws on

4. When ya drain the swamp, be careful what ya re-fill it with

5. If ya cop a feel, make sure ya pay em enough to shut up about it

6. Folks like made up stuff more than facts

7. Sticks and stones may break their bones but nick-

names will last ferever

8. It's as easy throwin folks under the bus as it is loadin em on it

9. Don't shortchange yer bus driver, he's gonna be one busy dude

10. Don't bother readin stuff if ya can catch it on Pox News

Abe asked Amos to read them back to him, and when Amos finished, Abe exclaimed, '*Oh*, that be soundin *perfect*, Amos!'

Amos was happy that he had the Ten Truths inscribed on the iPad and his face began to shine with a bright multicolored glow, similar to the aurora borealis, swirling around in both color and texture.

Abe looked at him and shuddered. 'Don't be lookin at me like that, Amos. Yer scarin the bejeezus out o meself. I'll need ya to be wearin a mask if yer gonna be like that!'

Amos drew his hand down across his face, and like magic the smile and light disappeared. He looked at Abe and said, 'Okay Abe, I don't want *ever* to be havin to wear a mask round all the time, hidin me happy, handsome face.'

Abe had never been so afraid in his life, and there had been plenty of times he had been scared. The tiger, the train, the missing ear, the alligators, just to name a few. Amos, his dear innocent brother, had morphed, changed into something different. He shuddered again as he looked at Amos, a transformed figure, a bold figure. 'Oh-oh!' he thought. 'Theo's figure, or at least Theo's figurehead.'

He kept his mouth shut as they made their way back to the tribe. When they arrived, Amos led them out of the burned-out forest back onto the great plains of Taxless towards the compound where Amos had saved Theo, in Maaco.

When they arrived in Maaco the tribe rebuilt the compound and finally settled down, happy that all the wandering was behind them. They still had their work cut out for them, though, building the Altar, so the milk and honey part would have to wait.

Theo had made it clear; he wanted an alter built in honor of himself. A place people could go into and pay homage to him. However, not being a detail guy, he had only given Amos some childlike sketches as to what it should look like.

Amos pondered the situation over and knew he needed some help getting the project under way, so he decided to talk it over with Abe. 'Hey, Abe. I gotta build an altar, and I need you to manage the construction.'

'Well, altarin-Amos, ya picked the right guy fer that. But why ya buildin that?'

'Oh, it's another one o Theo's hair-brained idears. He wants to have a place fer everybody herebouts to worship him.'

'Did he tell ya how to build it?' Abe asked.

'Well, he done said it had to be big enough to hold all o his precious belongings and have a place where everyone could use the restroom.'

'Who's gonna come to a place like that, Amos?'

'Don't worry bout that, Abe. This is gonna work out fine fer me. I got a plan to get me reputation back and make a tidy profit at the same time. And ya just gave me a fine idear what to call it – Altarin' Amos'. Now, take this sketch to an architect and then get some o those lazy-assed guys who be sittin about doin nuttin and set em to work.'

'Sure thing, Amos. I'll get right on that,' Abe said.

The work proceeded apace and when it was finished it looked more like a scaled down version of a domed sports arena than an altar.

Theo wanted the altar stocked with an endless list of accoutrements which included the most popular and fashionable items of the day, meaning oils, incense, herbs, and the like.

The altar, in fact, became an altar of altars. Amos, in the true

GUT spirit of the commercialization of everything possible, and forever on the lookout to turn a buck, set up a gift shop at the rear which the guests would be forced to exit through. He had every type of promo item known to the market, t-shirts, hats, stickers, buttons, even underwear.

Since the place was so large, he made sure it contained memorabilia and merch from almost every music and screen star who ever lived, along with every cultural GUT icon of the past and present.

The floor plan was simple enough. The rooms, or "chapels" as Amos called them, were set on the inside perimeter of the building, like concession stands in an arena. Each one, set side by side, contained items from the various themes.

There was the NBA Booth with autographed jerseys of Michael Jordan, the NHL Booth with Wayne Gretzky's hockey stick from the 1984 Cup final. Next along the line was the NFL Booth with Roger Staubach's autographed football from Superbowl VI, and then the US Open Tennis Booth with John McEnroe's autographed picture of him berating an umpire.

Moving along in a circular direction, counterclockwise (a motion hitherto unknown to most people in those parts) was the cinema booth, with posters of Marilyn Munroe, Humphrey Bogart, and Tom Voigt (in a previously unreleased photograph of him blowing Dustin Hoffman a kiss). There was also a signed photograph of the last of the great broads - Sharon Stone, and a slightly grainy photo of Jane Hathaway, well, to be precise, Nancy Kulp.

It went on from there, Disney with their adorably interactive Mickey and Minnie Mouse, Dunkin Donuts offering their delicious coffee and pastries, Denny's (where you could order a Cowboy Chopped Steak and Chorizo Burrito Combo for only $3.99), NASCAR (sporting a virtual racetrack for up to ten players), the WWE with robotic musclemen you could wrestle with, and even Macy's, of all things, selling giant caricature balloons of Amos.

The building was so large, some of the chapels were occupied by Gucci, Louis Vuitton, Hugo Boss, L'Oreal, Dior, Estee Lauder, Prada, and Yves Saint Laurent.

When Abe saw what Amos was doing he asked him, 'What are ya doin, Amos? Where's all the stuff Theo wants to put in here?'

'Don't worry, big brother, that's gonna go on the main floor, down yonder.' He pointed over the brass railing. 'See, there'll be a big Altar down in the middle where all Theo's stuff will be.'

Abe couldn't believe his eyes. 'Wow!' he exclaimed, 'Theo's gonna love that.'

'Right, but first I gotta get everything set up here so I can rise to fame again, just like afore.'

'Ye sure is a crafty one, Amos. Folks is gonna *love* this!'

'Yep, Abe, the way I see it, this here structure is gonna end up bein a magnificent tourist attraction. I been hearin that all the folks round these parts are God fearin patriots, and they'll go mad fer a place that combines pomposity with religiosity. And when that happens, my good name will be restored to what it was in Tango Sea.'

He remembered that Theo had been adamant on including a few other mysterious items, for some inexplicable reason. Things like a covenant box, a bread table, a lampstand, a bronze basin, and anointing oils. He also wanted it to contain incense and peppermints, and cluttered with thyme, red things, and many things that he couldn't find. He knew Abe was a resourceful opossum, so he asked him, 'Can you go out and try to find these things fer the altar. Here's the list.'

Abe looked at it and laughed. 'Cummon, Amos. He wants incense and peppermints, really?'

'Yepper, Abe, incense and peppermints, it'll be fine.'

It all made no sense, but for Amos it was all full of innocence, at the same time.

Abe wasn't impressed and said, 'That Theo is out o his cotton pickin mind. How we gonna sell any o that crappola? Next thing ye'll be tellin me is that he wants some crimson and clover in there, too.'

'I dunno, Abe, but I made room fer all o it anyway. And the

thing is, he just might strike me dead iffin I don't put it all on display.'

***

Theo had never factored in how far Amos would go with the altar, so he could not have imagined that the general public would be invited into it and that they would be there to worship *those icons* instead of him.

The altar went around and around, circling back to the NBA Booth, with sporadic breaks to allow concession stands selling popcorn, peanuts, hot dogs, squirrel-on-a-stick and, naturally, Budweiser on tap.

The place became wildly popular. Forget about fifteen minutes of fame. Amos became the man of the decade in less than a year. And when everyone found out he was the genius behind the Towering Trumpets outlets which now populated the whole country, he became an iconoclast, er, icon.

Amos started to shine, the pride of the south. He had become somebody everyone looked up to, both figuratively and literally, having stretched out to 6'3" and bulked up to 240 pounds.

He was indeed a towering trumpeter, and he said to Allbliss, 'Lookit me now, Ali-B. I done said afore I'd show all those rascally rascals what I truly got in me. And now they see it, I'm a billionaire!' (even though the real number was 240 million).

Allbliss knew what he was seeing, the glorification of a chosen one, a deity almost. He knew Amos had wanted to settle down with Fanny and the boys, but since he had returned from his search for Theo, he seemed much different. Amos appeared to have his old fire back. It made him think Amos might decide to run again for governor, and he knew that could be a good thing for his own fame and fortune, but it could be a very bad thing for a lot of people if he won. It brought to mind a somewhat obscure tune from way back in the early sixties by one of the kings of rock-and-roll, Buck Cherry. He involuntarily shimmied and shook when he recalled the lyrics, then laughed as he thought,

'C'est la vie.'

   ♫ He had a sky-high promo…girl, he sure made your feet tap
But he acted like a kid who's bored, someone shoulda gave him a slap
Cause if the vote comes round, you never know, it might go all to hell
So you see, it is no hoax, you're never sure how bad it might smell ♫

Chapter 38 - Amos Amalgamates The South

Theo had bigger plans for Amos than just having him build an altar where the tribe could worship him. He wanted Amos to free his people from oppression, and until Carmalita was destroyed, his tribe would never truly be free to live unmolested, by the authorities anyway. Theo contacted Krushin Krushelniski, who put him in touch with an expert group of computer hackers called No-namin-us. The hackers promptly enacted a plan to wipe out all traces of data from the DOH and DOHS computer systems about Amos and Abe's involvement in Mobie's murder, so Carmalita had no evidence to prosecute them with.

Early one evening Amos had fired up the barbeque out on his patio and was grilling a marinated snake. He chuckled at the coincidence of it when he heard the latest smash hit, "Light My Fire" by The Doors, playing on the radio. He flipped the snake over and began to smile, but his face clouded over when he heard the lyrics, which didn't sound like the original version.

♫ Some say that it can make you blue
   If you come across a burnin brier
   And from within someone says boo-boo
   And boy you're gonna lead the choir ♫

♫ Look here buddy in this brier
   Look here buddy in this brier
   You're gonna get to lead the choir ♫

♫ You'll shine as my mate, it's true
   Devine but hollow like a tire
   You'll lead them, no they can't refuse
   From above you'll be a federal friar ♫

♫ Look here buddy in this brier
   The one above the hollow tire
   You're gonna get to lead the choir

And make that Carmie take a flyer
Look here buddy in this brier
Look here buddy in this brieeeer ♫

He was scratching his head about the odd lyrics when a fire suddenly erupted in a tangled cluster of prickly vines nearby. He jumped up and rushed over to grab the water hose but heard a voice and stopped dead in his tracks. He looked around for a second and then heard the voice again.

'Boo-boo, Amos! Boo-boo, Amos Moses! I be needin onlyest one other thing from ya, googly-boy.'

Amos knew the voice immediately. It was Theo's voice, as clear as could be.

He called out, 'Where is ya, Pappy?'

'Lookit me here, in the burnin bush above the tire. Come closer, boy.'

Amos tried to peer into the bush, and he jumped back when he saw a tiny little face in the middle of the flames smiling at him.

'Great googly-woogly, Pappy. What the blazes is ya doin in there? Um, pardon the pun. What in tarnation is it with you and all the burnin vegetation, anywho? Ya done scared the bejeezuz outta me!'

Theo said, 'Pull yerself together, little spitter, and listen up good. There be one more thing I be needin ya to do.'

He laid out the plan for Amos to get the governorship of Taxless, amalgamate all the southern territories, and then run in the federal election to oust Carmalita from power. To convince him to run again for governor he reminded Amos of his past days of political glory in Tango Sea.

It made Amos feel for his people back home again. He was witnessing firsthand the benefits of a taxless economy right here in the Great Territory of Taxless. Taxless was so big and powerful that it had been able to get every penny back from GUT that they paid out in taxes, resulting in what they liked to call a "zero-sum game". He thought back to those crazy days with the amalgamated KKK and the people he had helped, how his business had expanded due to his notoriety, and then about all the money GUT had sucked out of him in taxes. And he knew he had the same level of notoriety now and was in a position to capitalize on his fame.

Theo said to him, 'Amos-ye-so-famous, it looks like ya really got that altar right, buildin it the way ye did. From the day ye wuz born I knew ya wuz a special child.'

'Yer right, Pappy, and thank ye,' Amos said. 'I thought it was gonna restore me good name, and it did, didn't it!'

'Yes, it surely did, son. Now listen up to what I be tellin ya. Yer a true towering trumpeter now and there ain't nobody better than yerself at blowin yer own horn. So, here's how it be. Ya gotta use the brands to yer advantage, now that ya got Altarin' Amos' to go along with The Towering Trumpets. It'll work just like last time in Tango Sea.'

'What about Carmalita, though?' Amos said. 'She be seriously after me hide.'

'I took care o that wrinkle a while back, so nobody's cummin after ye for nuttin.'

Amos was elated to hear the good news and be free of Carmalita's posse. 'You's a crafty one, Pappy. Ain't none I met was craftier, cepting mayhaps me.'

He was happy to be able to increase his popularity by running for governor, but he never, not for one second, thought about the effects that his policies of local tax reductions and regulatory repeals had had on the population in Tango Sea. The rapid expansion of food banks, the tenant evictions, the poor medical condition of the, well, the poor, or the children who were living on the streets. No, Amos was a positive guy, always looking on the bright side of life. As long as he had his comforts in life, he figured life should be good for everyone.

And he could see that Taxless was indeed a great promisin land, so he stepped up to the plate again to have another showdown with Carmalita. He figured that if he could secure the leadership of Taxless, he was sure the rest of the south would join him in battle. After all, he was still highly regarded in the

KKK, so once again he threw his MAGA hat in the ring for the Territorial election.

He decided to discuss with Abe and Allbliss what he intended to do, and the policy plans he would put forward.

**

During a morning breakfast meeting he said to Allbliss and Abe, 'Guys, I'z gonna run fer governor o Taxless and we be needin a strategy to convince all the voters to come o'er my way.'

'I kin help ya with that, Amos,' Abe said. 'First off, these folks is all farmers, so we gotta appeal to them. We gotta lay out all kinds o support fer them, ya know, like financin, distributin, shippin. Stuff like that thar. T'other thing be security, like building some kinda barrier to keep all the ne'er-do-wells outta herebouts.'

Allbliss was confused and a bit worried. 'What do you mean, Abe? If we barrier everything up, who's going to come to my concerts?'

'Don't ye be worryin bout a thing, Allbliss,' Abe said. 'We'd let em in fer yer shows.'

'Oh, okay then. That sounds fine to me, but the current governor could be hard to knock off. What's his name, Steve Outhausen, or something like that?'

Amos spoke up, 'I be likin that plan, Abe. Keep it simple-like and don't confuse anyone, least of all meself. And as far as Steve is concerned, don't worry too much bout him. I got his number.'

He hit the campaign trail running, well, sort of. He had gained a considerable amount of weight as he was not walking in the desert as much as he used to. And he was back living and, more to the point, eating, with Fanny. Neither he nor Fanny minded too much though, adding some more girth to his 6'3" frame.

Looking for a campaign manager, he said to Allbliss, 'You got the goods, Ali-B. All o the good folk out there think ye is a hunk a boilin lovin. I need ya to be one o me surrogates and win em all over to vote fer me. You up fer that?'

'I sure am, Amos. You know how I love to charm a crowd. I

might get Abe to help me with some strategizing, though.'

Amos said, 'Sure thing, he be as crafty as they come.'

Allbliss laughed. 'Yep, that opossum is on a first name basis with the bottom of the deck.' And then he thought, 'And best of all, I'll have a bigger name and wider market to strut my stuff.' And then he had another thought and asked, 'What are you gonna call the new amalgamation when you win over the southern territories?'

Amos smiled. 'I was thinkin about the "Great Ornery Patriots" Party.'

'Interesting choice,' Allbliss said. 'The acronym is something familiar to folks, something they would be comfortable getting behind.'

'Yer right about that Ali-B. So, get yerself out there and get the voters all riled up fer me cause.'

***

A debate with the territorial governor was arranged, and, remembering the Ten Truths, Amos continually referred to him by the nickname he had come up with, Stinky Steve. Steve wasn't about to take it lying down. During the chaotic debate, which degenerated into a mud-slinging contest, Steve finally blurted out a nickname he was loath to make public. 'Your policies are gonna turn us against each other and destroy our territory, Trumpty Dumpty.'

Amos was outraged that someone would dare make fun of him, and in public at that. He thought back to his days in Junior and Senior High, and how people had humiliated him. All the memories about how it made him feel came spewing out in an emotional, vitriolic rant. 'Yer makin fun o me, Thtinky Thteve? I ith thombody what never had no mammy, hardly ever had a thpeck o hair on me noggin, curthed with thethe googly eyeth, and on top o all them thtruggleth, I got thith infuriatin lithp by timeth. Ye, of all folkth, thhould ne'er be makin thport o me!'

Well, that was the clincher of the debate. People had always liked Amos, but they hadn't understood or even thought about the pain he had been through. The outpouring of support made itself known in both campaign donations and in the polls. Amos began gaining fast on Steve but still needed a strong final push to get him over the finish line.

Abe advised Allbliss to enlist the help of Kool Hands Kook to intimidate the opposition and suppress their voter registration efforts. Kook agreed to the plan but, unfortunately, being 93 years old, he found it difficult to book enough trips on the seniors' bus to be effective.

Abe hauled Allbliss aside. 'Listen, Kool Hands ain't doin much good fer us. He can only get out one day a week on the senior's bus.'

'Oh well, Abe, if it makes him feel useful, then what's the harm in that?'

The polling data indicated a tight race, so Amos had the idea that he should appear publicly as much as possible. When the crowds became excited, he did too, which sent him back now and again into his lisping. His fans didn't mind at all. They just seemed to love him all the more for it.

When election day arrived, Amos squeaked out a win, but sadly, Kook had died in a shoot-out at a voting booth over a dispute about a hanging chad. It hadn't been a case of him being too slow on the draw. Being a two-handed shooter who used the cross-over technique, he was used to having the gun-butts facing forward. However, having a touch of dementia by now, he had inadvertently slung his belt on backwards, that is to say from side to side, so the butts were facing *backwards*. Alas, the old codger, who could still shoot another man dead in the blink of an eye, went down in a hail of bullets. The southern DOHS had been called in to do an investigation, and their report contained only four words: Cause of Death - DOH!

Exhausted from the heavy campaign schedule and the stressful election, Amos was worn out when he attended Kook's funeral. He felt he needed a rest, so he took off with Fanny and the boys for a month at his Polo Ranch, which he named Polo-a-

Lago, even though there was no lake within a hundred miles of it.

After the month off, he returned and began to implement his platform promise to amalgamate the southern territories, with the goal of freeing his people from the oppression of the northeastern territories and bringing Carmalita to her knees.

He brought the territories together by pouring bucket loads of money into the farming communities, grain, beef, hog, and sheep alike. Amos' authority expanded in all directions, and he started to close off access to their territories with the beginnings of a barrier wall.

In the meantime, his supposedly most trusted supporters began skimming off money from the barrier wall funds and, one by one, were thrown into prison by a fierce federal prosecutor, Peter Uringal.

Amos approached Allbliss about the situation. 'Ali-B, I gotta get outta here fer a while. That Pissy Pete be throwin everybody in jail and I need to figure out how to squirrel me way out o his paws. That rascal Abe wuz doin some tricky stuff with the books that I gotta set to rights.'

'Good idea, Amos,' Allbliss said. 'Get away for a while, sort it out, and let the heat die down a bit.'

When Amos got the finances "adjusted" and he was free of Pissy Pete's grasp, he was excited for the opportunity to go *mano-a-mano* against Carmalita. But he never had a chance to hold any rallies against her. A pandemic struck the world, which Amos insisted was developed by a foreign enemy, Changpu Zhong, who was a former business associate of Theo's. Amos had previously cut off relations with Zhong, and Zhong was seriously jealous over the success of Amos' Altar. Zhong was a fierce competitor and widely known to hold private residences at exclusive addresses, including The Champs-Elysees, Piccadilly Circus, and Fifth Avenue (not to mention his sprawling resort on the outskirts of Bugtussle).

Amos went in search of Abe, wanting to get some advice on how to handle the response to the virus, but primarily how to exact revenge on Zhong. Abe suggested he enlist the help of a couple of retired bullfighters from southern Spain who were experts at the slicing and dicing game. Allbliss overheard the conversation and he recalled one of his favorite songs by Two Cloistered Occults, "Don't Fear the Creeper", and he began singing and wiggling around.

♫ Tallish crimes by one
    Zhong's....tryin to do us undone
    Reason won't scare that creeper
    But maybe twin bullfighters from Spain, oh they
    could go real far ♫

♫ Become deadly, they'll spear that creeper
    They will get that Zhong, they'll spear that creeper
    Put a sword in his eye, they'll spear that creeper
    Hey I know they caaaaaannnnnn ♫

♫ Haaa, ha-haaa, haaa-ha
    Haaa, ha-haaa, haaa-ha ♫

Amos laughed and called out to Allbliss, 'I be tellin ya, Ali-B, that connivin Way Downtown the Asian Clown, he started all this mayhem with the virus herebouts, and that's not a bad idear ya got there with them lyrics.'

Allbliss pulled out his comb and began to set his locks to rights, having been thrown askew after his manic gyrations. 'I just love that number, Amos. But seriously, what are you going to do about that virus? Everybody is starting to walk around bow-legged and hunchbacked because of it.'

Amos said, 'Those symptoms are nothin short of bedevilin and the most evil and nasty thing I ever seen. And ye been hearin what the treatment is? To help keep yer legs and backs straight, y'all gotta do a solo waltz twelve times a day facing northeastwards to the tune of "(You'll do it) My Way". How be that fer absolute blasphemy!'

'No, that can't be, Amos! Something sounds fishy about that!' Allbliss exclaimed.

'All I knows is what I done heard, Ali-B. That therapy was proscribed by the Centrifuge to Decrease the Colds. That group is in cahoots with those far-left radicals, sure nough. And I'll be tellin ya one thing more. I think it is all nothin but a hoax, in capital letters.'

'What do you mean, Amos?' Allbliss asked.

'We ain't gonna be dancing to the northeast, payin homage and actin all supplemental to them thar bleedin hearts, cause I think all this is gonna go away and everthin will be back to normalness in no time.'

He wanted to reassure his constituents that everything would be alright, so he held a news conference every day and repeated that the virus would disappear when the sun went down, which never came true. After several weeks, Abe convinced Amos, without providing a shred of evidence, that the treatment should be to eat Taxless chili dogs topped with guacamole sauce on even numbered days of the week.

It sounded like a good idea on two accounts to Amos. Firstly, he knew everybody liked chili dogs and guacamole, so that would, if nothing else, make them happy. And secondly, people spending all that money would help the economy.

He thought back to his college days and one of his economics courses. The class where they talked about the broader economy from a global perspective - Macro Economics. A perfect thought came to mind, and he thought he was quite clever, gifted actually, when he coined the term "Make-yer-Own Economics". It was a basic economic theory which promoted people spending their hard-earned money on products that were totally useless. But, of course, that wasn't the spin Amos put on it at his news conferences.

Chapter 40 - Amos Masks Up – Not!

Half the country was freaking out about the virus, and the other half either lived in abject squalor and didn't know about it, or simply didn't give a shit. Amos led the charge on the denier's side. He went on a highly publicized campaign to put the brakes on the terror that had gripped the nation. He began a furious Twitter feed that drew national attention.

> Amos Moses
> @theREALAmossofamous
> I'm a tellin ya, this is just another one o them thar HOAX's perpetualated by that dastardly president, Carmalita.
> 2:26AM

Then, after he stewed it over for a while:

> Amos Moses
> @theREALAmossofamous
> That Carmie is just tryin to git her grubby fingers into yer wallets, pertendin to need money to develop a vaccine. !!!FAKE NEWS!!!
> 2:31AM

And next, what he imagined was a perfect thought that came to him, one that could not be more perfect, in fact:

> Amos Moses
> @theREALAmossofamous
> Ye cain't see any virus floatin anywhere roundbouts. It only be another one o Carmalita's illusions to trick ye. !!! CONSPIRACY!!!
> 3:19AM

As the virus spread, the medical experts spoke with a unanimous voice, every group from the Centrifuge to Decrease the Colds to Hoppin' John's Universiality. Their message was clear, and they came up with what they thought was an effective, if somewhat frightening, hook – "Wear a mask to *slow the spread and reduce the dead.*"

The ad was highly publicized, ad nauseum (as far as Amos was concerned), and he reacted on Twitter as his base would expect.

> Amos Moses
> @theREALAmossofamous
> I got me own theory bout all everybody wearin them masks round town. Here be what I tell the coppers - Iffin ye cain't see their FACE, bring out the MACE!
> !!!STAND BACK and STAND BY!!!
> 4:32AM

Amos was on a roll by now, and it wasn't with Fanny. He was all hepped up and was ready for another attack. Wanting to roll out a new theme song, his "anthem" as he liked to think of it, he let her rip:

> Amos Moses
> @theREALAmossofamous
> Iffin yer hearin what I is tellin ya'll, ye otta hear what me dear sweet singer friend, Allbliss, put together. He did done a little re-writin on a Baby HaHa tune fer us, sumpin like an anthem, cause I knows we don't be needin our neighborly neighbors walkin round all masked up with poker faces. So, let's git our message out! - FOLLOW THIS LINK:
> www.j-j-j-joke-yer-lace-feed-my-base.doh!
> !!!SING IT OUT and SING IT PROUD, BOYS!!!
> 4:34AM

www.j-j-j-joke-yer-lace-feed-my-base.doh!

♫ We gonna scold ya, cause we're bold in Taxless Sea
   Those masks they gave us were too lacy, you see
   I'm so manly, more than any others could be
   Can't wear the mask, they'll call me lacy Lacey
   They's way too lacy, might even call me a she ♫

♫ Rant on high, say goodbye
   To that lacy lace, lacy lace
   Rant till nigh, say goodbye
   To that lacy lace, lacy lace ♫

♫ La-la-la-lacy lace, la-lacy lacy
   La-la-la-lacy lace, masks just ain't fer me ♫

Chapter 41 - An Asian Virus – Part 2

While the rest of the world managed to develop a vaccine and control the contagion, Amos' people suffered mightily. He refused to provide the vaccine to his people, fearing it was just another attempt by the well-known leftist vaccine developer, ANTUFA (the Antivirologists for a Utopia Free of Afflictions), to annihilate them.

Amos' people, with their severe bow-leggedness and pronounced hunchbacks, were unable to drive their vehicles, so they took to riding horses and electric bicycles with training wheels. By now Amos had accepted that the virus was real, and he was thrilled by *his* severe reaction to it when he contracted it. He proclaimed it a Theosend, as his bowed legs made it easier for him to ride his horse, and his hunchback made him more accurate in striking the polo ball at his Polo-a-Lago club.

That's not the way Allbliss saw things, though. The fans at his concerts were having difficulty dancing, that is, the ones who attended. The crowds were thinning out and he began to get concerned about the state of the economy, so he decided to have a chat with Amos.

'Amos, nobody has money to buy tickets to my shows because they can't work anymore. Their disability is crippling them up, and the economy, too. What are you going to do?'

'Much as I hate to do it, Ali-B, we be needin to get some foreign workers in here to pick up the slack.'

'You need to get this virus under control, too, Amos.'

'I know, I know. That Way Downtown the Asian Clown's virus is a killin us. Abe done told me about a feller who might be able to help us git that virus all cleaned up.'

'Who are you talking about?' Allbliss asked.

'Abe said the guy's name is Clean Hands Koreshenko. Apparently he is a Rasputinskian known fer his revulsion to filth. Seems like he has some type o cleanliness OCD. He kin clean everthin up all proper like.'

'Brilliant idea, Amos,' Allbliss said, 'you need to get right on that.'

Amos gave Abe the go-ahead to contract Clean Hands to clean the virus off all the public surfaces. Clean Hands' favorite choice of cleaners was ultraviolet light, but it was out of stock. The problem was that Amos had told everyone to use it to try and cure themselves, so there had been a run on it at the hardware stores. Alas, Amos hadn't been specific about which orifice to inject it into, which led to several peculiar and embarrassing moments in many households.

Clean Hands contemplated what to do and deduced that another type of light ray should work, selecting Gamma Rays. When he went to the hardware store, he loaded up his cart, and as he was in line waiting to pay for the products, he began quietly singing his favorite song. The cashier raised an eyebrow at the next customer in line and asked, 'Isn't that an old Neil Diamond tune he's tryin to sing?'

The lady said, 'I think so, Cracklin' Rosie, or sumpin like that. But the words seem a little off.'

The cashier responded, 'And that's not the onlyest thing that seems a bit off. Look at that tattoo on his neck, looks like a mop and a bucket or sumpin.'

They chuckled as Clean Hands continued to sing away, waiting his turn in line.

  ♫ Cleanin Korzie...wet that floor
     He's bout to hide all the virus round here by four
     It's gonna go
     He'll tell ya so ♫

  ♫ Wipe up that grime cause it sure is shady
     Itchin to get it bright again
     It's only he that will stop those spawns, oh-ho
     Cleanin along
     Even your thong ♫

♫ Cleanin Korzie's a floor mop footman
And he can clean when he starts to brushin
Then cranks it in swirls
That virus just don't belonnnggg ♫
♫ Spray it out
Spray it out
Spray it out, dear Korzie ♫

The cashier interrupted him, 'Hey, mister! Yer next, and I think you got those lyrics all scrambled up, mayhaps like yer brain is.'

He stepped up to pay for the products and noted, 'I think I see a speck o dirt on your lapel, young lady.'

She reached over and slapped him in the face and, as she swirled an open palm in front of her chest, said, 'The onlyest thing ye need to be worryin bout is payin, buddy, so keep yer leerin eyes offa me upper torso area.'

Clean Hands promptly paid her and dashed out of the store. When he applied the Gamma Rays to the buildings, he realized that he should have used Hydrosuperclean (which he rejected because it smelled too much like gasoline), because the Gamma Rays damaged all the surfaces he applied them to.

Amos was incensed with the turn of events, with yet another of Abe's schemes gone awry. 'Darn good thing he didn't use it on the citizenry, Abe! Now we gottta fix up all the buildins.'

'Leastwise there's lots o work fer everybody, little brother.'

'How stupid kin ya be, ya twisty varmint. Not only did you make me look stupid again, but nobody is able to work, and it's gonna break our bank payin a bunch of foreign workers to git the work done!'

Chapter 42 – The Wheels On The Bus Go Round And Round

The temporary workers were brought in, thankful to have their feet on GUT soil. But Abe, hopeful to get back into Amos' good graces, arranged to double tax them to reduce the cost.

Allbliss always invited fans backstage after his shows, and that's where he discovered their discontent. By now, everyone knew about the raw deal the temporary workers were getting. And they knew about all the money that was pouring in from sales at the Altar. How could they not, the parking lot was filled to overflowing every day.

The foreign workers began to protest peacefully in the streets about the state of their destitution. They couldn't just get up and leave. The Beautiful Barrier Wall was heavily guarded, and they would be denied exit.

Allbliss was none too happy himself, but not about the same thing they were grumbling about. He had had enough of Abe's mismanagement of everything. He thought back to the failed negotiations with Carmalita, to the plagues, to Mobie's demise, and now this latest fiasco with Clean Hands Koreshenko. He approached Amos and said, 'Amos, I'm telling you we might have a revolution on our hands here. Those protesters are highly ticked off with you, and it's really all Abe's fault.'

'I know it's true, Ali-B, but what kin I do?'

'Well, I don't think it's safe for you to be out wandering around too much. To get things settled down, why don't I take over the public speaking again. I'll charm and wiggle them, just like last time.'

'Ya might be needin a new act this time. Ya know, wow em with somethin else,' Amos suggested.

'Oh, I've got an idea on that, alright. I figure some nice glittery outfits and a few new head moves will do the trick,' Allbliss said.

Amos nodded, 'Ya might have somethin there, Ali-B. I think

that might work.'

After Allbliss held a few free concerts, he scheduled a news conference where he announced that Amos was considering sending in the Conglomeration of Guards to disperse the protesters. In response, as a show of good faith, the protesters began to work around the clock scrubbing the outside of every GOP building with Hydrosuperclean to show their support for the territory. The leader of the guards, Georgina Custard (yes, the same one from the Tango Sea fiasco) whom Abe had secretly brought over during the tribe's exodus, believed they were saturating the buildings with gasoline in order to light them on fire. Fearful for the safety of her guards, she called in the Fire Department, who sprayed the buildings with high-pressure jets of water. The protesters dispersed, leaving behind building facades which were shimmering and shining in the late afternoon sun.

'What in tarnation happened there, Ali-B?' Amos asked. 'We look like fools with all o them ridiculous hijinks. The protesters ended up lookin like the heros, gittin our buildin's all clean and shiny.'

'That was all on Abe, Amos. He's the leader of the guards, and that Georgina, remember her from Tango Sea? She always was a problem. I don't know why he keeps promoting her, but I have my suspicions.'

'Well, looks like it's time to get the bus warmed up. That Cain't-Cut-the-Mustard Custard has gotta go! And I'll be tellin ya this, Abe ain't far behind her.'

Allbliss just smiled and licked his lips, thinking about returning to his favorite meal.

***

A national election was scheduled for the following year and the economy was in tatters, due in part to Carmalita's liberal tax-and-spend policies, trying to recover from the devastating financial effects of the virus.

Amos figured he should automatically receive the national party nomination to run for President of GUT in the upcoming election, since he was so well known on the national stage. But he had to secure the party nomination in the Primary run-off, so he developed a campaign platform which included distributing credits for free Polo playing lessons at his resorts all over the country. He also was going to offer free electric bicycles and horses for everyone, and one year's supply of Taxless chili dogs and guacamole sauce.

Abe argued vehemently against this approach with Amos. 'Now looka, I say, looka here, Amos-ain't-so-contagious, that strategeum ain't gonna work round these parts. Those northern folks ain't got no more polo sense than they got sensibilities how to git a hot bull off a heffer in heat. And they ain't bent over and all wobbly-kneed like us folks down here, so they don't have any mobility issues. But hey, keep the chili dog thingy.'

Amos was fed up with Abe and said, 'Don't be a sellin me idears short, short-tailed-Abey. Ye ain't been such a hot bull yerself lately, I been observin, hardy-har-har!'

'Listen up, ya disrespectin youngin, what they be needin is a strong program of Lawn Order. That be the big thing these days, Amos, with all o this lootin and riotin goin on herebouts.'

'Yer right, Abe. Folks is all gung-ho for law and order these days. Mayhaps I'll include that in me program.'

Abe corrected him, 'No, no, no, Amos. It be a program of free lawn and garden care that'll help the disabled constituents improve their properties after all o this mayhem gets settled down.'

Amos became infuriated. 'Now that thar ith the motht idiotic thing ye ever came up with, and ye've come up with a whole pile o idiotic thingth in yer dayth. Ya keep talkin tho thilly I might jutht cut off yer other ear. Every plan ye ever hatched to make me look good all turned out the other way round!'

It dawned upon Abe that Amos was really starting to lose it, so he again used the strategy of playing dead, but Amos didn't fall for the trick this time either, and booted him across the floor.

Abe got up and, rubbing his ribs, warned him, 'You better be sleepin with one eye open from here on in, Amos. I got me some nasty friends lurkin round and they might just be gettin even with ya fer that thar move.' He jumped up on the kitchen counter and after he leaped through the window, Amos heard him howl when he landed on the hot barbeque.

Amos had finally hit the wall with Abe and went in search of Allbliss to tell him to take Abe out of the picture. He found him over at Alice's restaurant and was happy to see him in exceptionally good spirits, singing the latest hit by Wanderin Stevie.

♫ I'm so so so suspicious, that possum's full of gall
　I'm so so so suspicious, Abe's about to crawl
　I'm so so so suspicious, what's that possum still
　doin here
　I'm so so so suspicious, he'll be dead in less a year ♫

♫ But that crazy ole possum, ohohohohoh
　He be dead in less a year ♫

♫ If ye........♫ 'HEY, Ali-B!' Amos interrupted. 'Whatcha doin there?'

'I think I have an idea for a song, Amos.'

'If those lyrics are it, we cain't be waitin a whole year to get that squirrely possum out o the picture, iffin that's what yer getting at, Ali-B,' Amos said.

'I sure had that critter in mind when I was making up them lyrics. If you want to get rid of him, just tell me what it is you want me to do.'

'Well, don't be eatin him. Just call the bus driver and git him as far away from this place as ya can. I don't be wantin any trouble from that scurrilous little devil anymore.'

'I'll get right on that, Amos. You can count on me,' Allbliss assured him.

***

Allbliss managed to capture Abe with a net and put him in a cage. Abe was howling like a banshee when Allbliss tossed him into the back of the bus.

Abe squeaked, 'Where ya takin me, Allbliss?'

'You've got a one-way ticket to Ipanema, Abe. We've had enough of your disastrous plans.'

Abe was getting twitchy and thought about it for a second. 'They got any possums in them parts?' he asked.

'I don't know about opossums, Abe, but you might find a nice girl down there. But if not, I'm sure you'll have a good time at their Hippie Feria that goes 24/7.'

After a few minutes Abe realized he needed to get control of the situation. He was sure he could sweet-sing Allbliss out of being cruel to him, since he had been so true to him over the years, even penning his top selling songs.

'Hey, bold-Blissy,' he said, 'I got new, more better words to go along with the song ya sung over at the Mrs. Pippi River, "Crossin the Divide", member that one? That disco stuff is popular again, so I wrote this one fer ya last Saturday night whilst I wuz in an awful fever, hardliest even knew if I wuz gonna stay alive. Here's the lyrics, try em out.' Allbliss was intrigued and told the bus driver to pull over to the side of the road. He tuned his iPhone into the melody and began to sing it out.

♫ See that Amos risin, but all the folks is cryin
   He is makin em cry, makin em cry
   The reason they is cryin is from all his virus lyin
   They can barely survive, barely survive
   Strive to drive, strive to drive, barely survive, barely survive
   Strive, strive, strive, strive, he is makin em cryyy-
   yyy-yyy-yyy ♫

'That sounds like a good one too, Abe, with a melody everybody loves!'

'Yepper, wrote it after I saw yer bendy legs spinnin round like a disco ball. It'll be great fer yer act.'

'Wow! You're right, Abe. I was thinking about jumping on the Disco train.'

'Nother thing I is right about, Allbliss, is what yer doin here now ain't right. Yer the one who got the goods to run the big show and knock that Amos offa his pedestrial.'

Allbliss squinted at Abe and said, 'So that's what the song is about.'

'Yep,' Abe said, 'sure as shootin it is. And ya kin use it in the Primary run-off against Amos. Then everybody will be wantin to go to your rallies and concerts.'

Allbliss thought back to how he had seen Amos transform, and how it had scared him, and how the people had suffered in Tango Sea under Amos' governorship. And then he thought about Theo.

'I think you have a good idea there, Abe,' he said.

***

He was getting in an upbeat mood, thinking how he could have another big hit with Abe's new song. He got out of the bus and started singing and dancing away, hips a-swiveling and bowlegs flapping around like a Tasmanian devil.

Abe, seizing the opportunity, convinced Allbliss some trickery would be required to sway the population over to win the primary contest against Amos. Allbliss, who was excited about having a new hit song, dismissed all of Abe's previous failures and agreed to the plan. He told the bus driver to turn around and they headed back home.

Knowing about Changpu Zhong's distain for Amos, Abe conspired with Way Downtown to come up with some creative campaign messaging promoting Allbliss as the legitimate leader of the GOP Party.

Way Downtown, not knowing about Stinky Steve's previous mistake, decided to focus on Amos' deficiencies, his hair implants, his speech impediment, his googly eyes, and his expanding girth, instead of highlighting Allbliss' qualities.

Amos managed to discredit Allbliss at his rallies by relying on something tried and true, mudslinging. 'Listen up, y'all. That Allpiss-and-no-vinegar ain't nuttin but a fallen rock star and former convict. Hardy-har-har! His biggest hit wuz True Made Blues, and ye know where that come from? It wuz a tribute to a blue jeans manufacturing facility owned by none other than his buddy *Way Downtown the Asian Clown*! So there ye have it, Mister Allpiss is just a puppet of our Asian archenemy and that corrupt opossum, who ye all knows bout by now.' He'd then look off-stage for dramatic effect and bellow out, 'Sierra, Sierra Huckleberry! You over there? Call the bus driver, pronto!'

Allbliss never had a chance. Amos won the primary contest, hands down, to lead the GOP in the election campaign against Carmalita.

Chapter 43 - A Battle Cry For Amos

Allbliss placed a video call to Amos to congratulate him on his win. 'I am so sorry for doubting you, Amos, but I'm happy that you're getting your good name back.'

'Aww, Ali-B, don't worry bout a thing. We been friends fer too long to let sumpin like that to get betwixt us.'

As sincerely as possible Allbliss said, 'Why, thank you, thank you very much, Amos. You know, of course, it was Abe who sent me off on that ridiculous campaign.'

'Yep, Ali-B, I know. But it's hard to hold it against him either, being me brother and all.'

'Right, I understand. But listen, I toiled day and night over a song I wrote for you, kind of a medley. And because you're so different, I thought I'd switch the tempo and rhythms around from verse to verse, you know, to make it as unique as you are. It's about how eventually you're going to get that nemesis of yours, Carmie, for the way she's been acting like a Queen all the time and lording it over us from up on high. It's not quite finished but I'll sing you a few verses to give you an idea of how it goes. It's called "A Battle Cry For Amos".'

Amos looked in wonder at Allbliss and said, 'That sounds awesome, Ali-B. Ya actually wrote a tune yerself, and it's just fer me!'

'I did, Amos, believe it or not. Here, I'll sing what I've got so far.'

He had never seen Allbliss so inspired as he began singing the most unusual song. It was the oddest arrangement of what he thought was a rock ballad combined with a bohemian influenced opera. It was strange indeed, how the melody kept changing with each verse, but there was something catchy about it, and ominous, too. With his hips a-swiveling and his upper body contorting, Allbliss turned on the soundtrack and belted out the tune.

♫ He's a thriller, and mean
   Amos, a modern Philistine
   Such a googly-boy you've never seen
   He is gonna save our kind
   We'll be fine ♫

♫ Bum budda lum ba da lumbah
   Dee dee die do day
   Pleasure....shoving me aside
   Givin the tax to her, leavin none fer me
   Pleasure....we cain't find nowhere
   She took it all away, he'll knock her off her feet
   Pleasure....Amos we need pleasure
   Pleasure....where do we find pleasure ♫

♫ He's a thriller, and mean
   Amos, a modern Philistine
   His fake hair, just watch him preen
   He is gonna save our kind
   We'll be fine ♫

♫ Your game, sort of, of taxing us all into a fit
   Your game, sort of, we will never get used to it
   He is steadyyyyyyy
   Give her a little fling and shove ♫

♫ He's a thriller, and mean
   Amos, a modern Philistine
   He has every perfect gene
   He is gonna save our kind
   We'll be fine ♫

♫ Aww...she's all take and no give
   Every time Carmie takes tax from we
   She needs we....in order to live
   Aww, he'll take her life now, sonny

Yes, he'll give her the shiv ♫
♫ He's a thriller, and mean
Amos, a modern Philistine
A wizard with the latest meme
He is gonna save our kind
We'll be fine ♫

♫ Carmie, yer a bad gal, nasty gal
Takin all our taxes, he'll take em back one day
Ye'll have crud in yer lace, you're mostly two-faced
He's gonna make ya disgraced one day ♫

♫ He's a thriller, and mean
Amos, a modern Philistine
He'll give her a hard regime
He is gonna save our kind
We'll be fine ♫

♫ Don't let that girl survive, Amos
Don't let that girl survive
Aww, whatever you contrive, Amos
Be sure you make her cry ♫

Amos was beside himself with glee and he began clapping. Allbliss just nodded his head and said, 'Thank you, thank you very much.'

The song excited and inspired him, so he said to Allbliss,' That be the thweetetht thong I ever done heard, Ali-B. Ye otta record that one and git it on the radio. All me adorin fanth will love the way it maketh me thound tho tough and powerful, not to mention how I will free em from oppreththion.'

Allbliss beamed with delight and said, 'I already got a start on that. I figure we can play snippets of it at your rallies to remind them how you're going to bring Carmalita down and set them free.'

'Dandy idear, Ali-B. I love it, love it, LOVE IIIIIIT!'

The recording sessions were completed the following week

and the southern radio stations latched onto the song like a hawk onto an opossum. Allbliss had another chart-topper on his hands and was looking forward to singing it to support Amos at his concerts and at Amos' rallies.

Wanting to project a strong image, Amos had intended to make his national debut in front of the media by gliding down the escalator at his flagship building, Trumpeting Tower, with his family in tow. The sad fact was that the escalator got jammed halfway down.

The massive cheering crowd began to speculate as to the problem. Some believed it to be the combined weight of Amos (now clinically obese), Fanny, and the twins, who had by now grown to rival their father's girth. Others thought it looked like the rolling handrails were bending outward and the emergency system had kicked in to shut the escalator down.

One way or the other, they managed to unceremoniously jostle their way to the bottom and kicked off Amos' campaign with much fanfare.

Desperate to get back into Amos' good graces, Abe figured he would act as a surrogate to support Amos' campaign. He decided to bring in someone he thought could help win Amos over, so he held a dance party and invited Amos' most beloved performer, Mean Gene the Dancing Machine. Amos was elated and, seeing that it was his brother, took Abe back into the fold to help him in the upcoming GUT election for the presidency of all the territories.

When the election polls were released, they showed that Amos was losing badly with all demographics except the severely contorted Polo players. He insisted that his own polls showed the exact opposite, but Abe convinced him to begin a campaign strategy focused on diversifying his base.

'I be tellin ya what ya needs to do to win this thing, Amos. Ya needs to be gettin out and speakin at rallies day and night.'

Amos agreed, but on the fourth day, in Squeezie-Anna, he became severely dehydrated. Abe suggested he drink a magic elixir to help him rehydrate, so he took Amos over to meet his voodoo mama in Two-Animes. Finally, it appeared something Abe did worked the way it was supposed to. Well, kind of, anyway. Amos rebounded, but it turned out that the cocktail also contained a critical element of every love potion ever concocted (puree of opossum gizzard) and was locally known as "Number 9". After gulping down a healthy dose, Amos rose from the chair and broke out into song.

♫ I brung my achin o'er to Madman Sooth
He had a table in a nipsy's booth
He took my cash and everything was fine
When he sold me an elixir of
"Hair-combin All-the-time" ♫

The effect was stunning. Amos' heart filled to bursting with love for the first person he saw after drinking the potion. Regrettably, Madman forgot to cover the mirror that was next to Amos, which was the first thing he looked at, and he fell in love *with himself*! Like his best buddy Allbliss, he began to constantly look in the mirror and comb his beautiful full head of wispy blond hair.

He said to Abe, 'I knows what we be needin now, Abe. We gotta get all o me faithful out into the nation and spread the word, ya know, git some herd mentality goin on. Get that Ali-B back in with us to sing that captivatin song he done wrote bout me. Me fans all love that one.'

Abe said, 'That be the dangdest plan I ever did hear, Amos. Ye got the real boldness in yerself now, brother. Ye keep up yer speakin tours and I'll git onta that thar angle and start bookin events fer Allbliss and all yer surrogates.'

***

Amos opened each of his speaking engagements full of rage for Carmalita's supporters. He ranted and raved about all her loyal bleeding-heart socialist cronies who were helping her snatch every last nickel of taxes possible from everyone to enact her social policies.

With fireworks and flash bombs firing off in all directions, the booming beat of the music helped inflame his adoring fans. The music would rise and fall in concert with Amos' speech, somewhat akin to a revivalist sermon. His fans would clap, chant, and holler out in unison or individually, whenever a moment struck them as particularly inspiring, or at times laughable. And he would finish by making it clear that he was their savior, but he would need both their votes and their campaign donations to help them achieve their dream. The closing song captured the theme perfectly with a call to action from one of his favorite Rap artists, M&M.

♫ Failure's dark world is comin up on their side
Up on their side, up on their side ♫

♫ Yes, he'll attack
But he needs friends
Amos'll attack
Callin all men ♫

♫ Gather round him, and holy gee
He'll tell ya xactly how to please he
Make them cry, put them on their knees
But ya cain't save yer taxes by excluding he ♫

♫ Press and attack
Don't be slack
Press and attack
Dress in black
Press and attack
Bring a bat
Press and attack
Give em a whack ♫

At every rally, Amos consistently hammered away on two topics – denigrating ANTUFA and his opponent, Carmalita. He repeated the speech over and over, word for word, at every rally. After his third or fourth rendition it was obvious to everyone that he should have used either a better speech writer, or tried a little decaf, maybe even some meditation tapes, as he tended to get all hepped-up and over-emotional.

'Now y'all lithten to me, and lithten up good. That Carmalita Beelzebubita (with the song "Black Magic Woman" rising in the background) be in cahootth with that evil group ANTUFA (and now the song "Evil Woman" rising), well, y'all know who I mean. They be the two devilth who is violatin our right to freedom. Beelzebubita (now the song "Witchy Woman" rising) ith denyin our right to protetht in public and I think her agentth are the people who ith thneakin around doin all the lootin and torchin o the buildingth!' The crowd roared in agreement, firing off several rounds with their shotguns.

'We all knowth that Beelzebubita ith incompetent and too old to run thingth. With her old jalopy walker, how will that nathty woman ever git from point A to point C, er, - B cometh next, don't it? Anywho, her brain ith mo nattery than that o an opoththum bein thkinned alive, er,' he hesitantly looked offstage at Abe, 'thorry bout that dear brother. What I ith tryin to thay ith that her cognitivity be all thcrambled up.'

With the excitement building, his supporters went wild, firing off an array of Roman Candle and Bottle Rocket fireworks. The crowd rose to their feet and chanted his name when Amos invited Allbliss to the stage to sing a few verses of "A Battle Cry For Amos".

♬ He's a thriller, and mean
    Amos, a modern Philistine
    Deadly as a serpentine
    He is gonna save our kind
    We'll be fine ♬

♬ She is darn right full o lust
    Grabs our taxes and we are bust
    She is gonna go down, she is gonna go down
    He'll bust that bitch, he must ♬

♬ He's a thriller, and mean
    Amos, a modern Philistine

A saviour full of self-esteem
He is gonna save our kind
We'll be fine ♫

♫ Amos...he has got a plan
Lay a bomb next to her bed
Push the button, she'll be red
Carmie, it sure seemed like fun
Too bad we had to end it up that way ♫

♫ He's a thriller, and mean
Amos, a modern Philistine
He's a being so Supreme
He is gonna save our kind
We'll be fine ♫

♫ Our kind is the champaigns, in the end
We'll pop the cork, and we'll transcend
See, nothin like us champaigns
Nothin like us champaigns
Clocks tick fer schmoozers
Nothin like us champaigns
O'er that girl ♫

The audience roared again and when the cheering and applause died down, Amos continued his rant, 'And that ain't the quarter o it all. There be thumpin funny bout the birthin o that nathty woman. I been thinkin thomebody otta be lookin into that hair-brained thtory bout her bein born up north in The Great Territory of I'll-Ask-Ya. Carmalita otta come out and *prove* that, mayhapth even produthe her birthin thertificate to thomebody herebout!'

Amos felt the adrenaline pumping. 'And another thing, the ANTUFA agentth ith tryin to make it look like it was uth provokin all the mayhem, when it ith really them!'

He wrapped up the show on a high note, calling Carmalita a danceless dunce (which never quite rolled off his tongue smoothly) with the crowd cheering and chanting to the sound of "Juke Box Hero" blaring at full volume.

***

After the success of the previous rallies, Abe thought it would be a good idea to organize a type of reality show which pitted two teams against each other in a format that was as brilliant as it was fundamental to people's perception of the world. Well, to Amos' base, anyway.

It was played out in gameshow fashion to kick off every rally. One team would be the "Good Guys" and the other team would be the "Bad Guys". The participants were selected from the crowd and, as everyone knew it was just for fun, they eagerly agreed to join in. The themes were simple enough and rotated on alternate nights.

The "Hard Workin Team" versus the "Lazy Bums Team"

The "Forestry Team" versus the "Tree-Hugger Team"

The "Tariffin Team" versus the "Sell the Farm Team"

The "Each Man fer Hisself Team" versus the "Regulatin Team"

The winners on each night were selected by Amos, who would declare at the end, 'YE IS HIRED!'

The losers would have their heads shaved bald by the winners (which was, without fail of course, the good guys). The only problem they had was that most of the participants were bald to begin with. Still in all, everyone had a good big laugh out of the shenanigans and got them in a good mood for Amos' speeches.

At the rally in Shatnopoopoo, Amos surveyed the crowd and noted three people in the front row cheering wildly wearing MAGA hats. People he recognized from high school. Cruisin Ted, Marc-Oh!, and Dandy Rand-ee. He gave them a disdainful "*I told you so*" smirk, wiggled his finger at them to come up on stage, and assigned them to the Lazy Bums Team.

As the rallies went on, Amos continued to hammer away at the two themes, Carmalita's infirmities and ANTUFA's subterfuge. But he wasn't done there. As his confidence grew, he decided to throw caution to the wind.

He noticed lately that Carmalita was having difficulty finding the precise words that had come to her so easily in the past. They were just minor hesitations, really, but they *were* noticeable. Amos seized on the opportunity, remembering like it was yesterday, back to the taunts of his childhood. He delivered the blow at the subsequent rally and blasted her with it every chance he got.

'I'm a tellin ya, that Babbalita is loothin her marbleth. That nathty woman cain't put two and two thoughtth together and git three. Kin hardly even git the wordth outta her mouth proper-like. I'm ponderin her quacky doctor hath got her on thumpin to keep her engine fired up. I think that woman otta do what I done to prove her cognitability. I took a tetht, a *really hard* tetht. And here'th how it wuz. Me phythi, er, doctor, done give me three words to be rememberin, and I had to remember em fer a *long time*. Like I'm talkin five minuteth er thix, and then I had to tell em back to him.'

'They wuz hard wordth, too, and all double wordth to boot, like Poththum Thtew and Thkewred Giththardth. The latht one wuz from a tune I never heard in ageth – Rebel Rebel. Thuited me perfect-like though, don't ya think!' He winked and the crowd cheered in agreement, and he continued, 'I wuz tho perfect at it, and the doc thaid no one wuz ever tho perfect, like I wuz a genial, or thumpin like that thar. I want Babbalita to try that one on fer thize. Ain't no way that nathty woman kin do it.'

The crowd began to chant repeatedly, 'Amos, Amos, yer the one can save us.'

Abe picked his moment to inject some high voltage energy into the event, cranking up ABCD's latest smash hit to full volume.

♫ Ye knows a woman and yer needin her gonged
Mayhaps ye've too small nuts
Takin yer taxes in every single way
Just like the other sluts

Get out o her zone
Ring me and moan
I'll wait fer yer chime
I'm at
666 666 9
Ya know I'm so sublime ♫

♫ Nasty seed, make her weep
Nasty seed, make her weep
Nasty seed, make her weep
I'm a nasty seed, and I'll make her weep ♫

Amos sucked up the crowd's adulation and smiled. He had them in the palm of his hand, and that's when he knew it was time to lay out his next attack, something more outrageous than he, or anyone, had ever done before.

Even though his bowlegs had not completely straightened out yet, and still looking somewhat like Quasimodo, his adoring fans let loose a mighty cheer while he was basking in glory on stage. Feeding off their adoration, he ripped off his shirt to reveal a Hulk Hogan T-shirt underneath. He wanted them to know he had beaten the virus and how strong, REALLY STRONG, he was. The music track blared out to the latest Mike's-all Jackin hit, and he invited Allbliss back onto the stage to sing the lyrics. The crowd went berserk when he approached the microphone, belting out the song in a tour-de-force performance for the mash-up.

♫ Defeat it, defeat it
Defeat it, defeat it
Only a guy like he
Could defeat it
And he'll Tweet it
Yeah, he'll Tweet it ♫

The crowd went wild, and he continued.

♫ We ain't gonna be mistreated
See he is chunky, and how he just might

Give that nasty girl, the fight o her life

Must Tweet it, yeah, just Tweet it ♫

By that point everybody was rockin and rollin, and joined in singing with their arms raised, phones lit up, and swaying to the rhythm.

♫ Tweet it, Tweet it

Tweet it, Tweet it

Git yerself up

And re-Tweet it

Yeah Tweet it, Tweet it

Tweet it, Tweet it ♫

Needless to say, all the videos of the event went viral on Twitter, Tic Tok, You Tube, and even K-Pop Channel, and every system crashed shortly thereafter.

**

Wanting to take advantage of Amos' notoriety, Abe seized the moment. The latest fad was Town Hall events, so he booked Amos into a session at Gator Fame University. Abe was wise enough to pre-select the audience, and he had given them questions to ask Amos. There wasn't much he could do about the moderator, who had been selected by the Dean. She was untouchable, a beacon of journalistic integrity.

The event started off cordially, with the moderator, Samantha, offering polite introductions and then setting the rules of procedure.

She then opened the debate. 'Amos, all the previous presidents served in the military in some capacity. Why haven't you done the same, seeing as you want to become the Commander-in-Chief?'

'Well, sweet girl, when I received my draft notice, the doctor diagnosed me as having a cronic case of severe toejamitis.'

'Hmm, I've never heard of that before, Amos, and I was a health reporter for ten years previous to this assignment. But let's move on to my next question. It appears your policies don't account for supporting anyone who is struggling in our country. What is your philosophy on that?'

Amos responded, 'Ha, and hardy-har-har to boot! That Beelzebubbita's been tryin desperatmost to help a bunch o lazy-ass folk who ain't no good fer nuttin anyways. She is nuttin but a nasty woman and she ain't gonna do anybody herebouts any good a'tall.'

Samantha then invited a question from the audience, 'Hi, famous-Amos. Thanks fer invitin me.' Amos stroked his golden locks and smiled as she continued, 'There be a bunch o crazy talk bout conspiracies goin on herebouts lately, like some evil doers tryin to rig the election. Who be those folks and what in tarnation is that thar all bout?'

Amos sat up with a furrowed brow, looking like he had a deep understanding of the issue, and said, 'Darned iffin I knows anything bout them thar shenanigans, honey-pie. All's I be knowin is that they all seem to love yer's truly. That bein me, o course!'

Samantha broke in, 'But Amos, they are the groups who are trying to divide our nation, along with the Opaque Supermostomists. Aren't you concerned about that?'

Amos was caught off guard, thinking the event was going to be a cakewalk. He began to get nervous and fidgeted in his chair, but thought he was a clever constitutionalist when he fired back, 'I ith, I truly ith worried. Iffin they got thumpin to thay, then they got a right to thay it under the conthti... er, well, ye know, the law. And iffin they bow down to me all adorin-like, then I thay, thtep up and thtep onwordth!

Samantha largely took control of the remainder of the event, going through the long list of groups who she felt were a threat to the nation: the Loud Noise, the Oat Eaters, Do-A-Con, the Boverine Botch Dawgs, and the Three Pretenders, only to name a few. Well, it was clear where it was headed from there. It descended into a bitch-fight, a no-holds-barred cage-match, with one attempting a scissor-kick while the other tried a pile-driver, all involving the highest heights of drama, with not the least bit of substance anywhere to be found.

But Amos, gaining more confidence as the audience cheered him on, ended on a high note in his final, highly emotional rant, 'Ye ith one nathty woman, Thamantha, and I never did witnethth in all me born dayth anyone nathtier. Them thar quethionth ye athked me wuz evil, thame ath ye ith. And iffin ye weren't tho goll-darn pretty I'd be whackin ye upthide yer head with a lead pipe. Probly thayin "Great Googly Woogly" at the thame time!'

Samantha was aghast at the outburst but wrapped up the session and thanked him for his spirited participation. She came out from behind her desk and as Amos extended his hand, she, being steadfastly committed to freedom of expression, swiftly kicked him in the nuts.

Carmalita found it hard to compete, and not only on the technology front. Being a septuagenarian by now, she needed a walker to help her get around, and had trouble keeping up to the heavy travel schedule. Her mental acuity was never questioned by her doctors, but she *had* lost half a step now and again when it came to her legendary wit. She had heard about the things Amos was saying about her, so she decided to address the issue up front.

She challenged Amos to a duel of wits at sunrise on Smythe Street, but Amos was so excited that he wrote it down as Thmythe Thtreet. The next morning as the massive crowds were gathered along both sides of the street, Amos was late for the showdown because of his search for a street that didn't exist. This gave Carmalita, while waiting with her café mammaduchay with whipped cream caramel and a cherry on top, the opportunity to enthrall the crowds with a gut-wrenching rendition of Mobie's "My Gift Today", a song dear to the hearts of every GUT citizen from north to south. By the time Carmalita sang the last note, there wasn't a dry eye in the crowd, with everyone thinking about Mobie's sweet voice and the horror of what had happened to him.

When Amos arrived, Abe, in yet another act of lunacy, suggested a game of wordplay. He thought that Amos had become a linguistic giant, and to be fair to the scruffy rodent, so did all of Amos' supporters. Amos was mesmerizing when he spoke, to be sure, but the truth was he never said anything, or at least anything of substance.

So, the game was chosen and true to form, Abe fucked it up again. It was bad enough that he stipulated in the rules that the first player to use the letter "s" more than twice would lose the game. And it didn't help that he had given Amos, on the advice of George Clooney (not realizing that George was a die-hard supporter of Carmalita) a triple caffeine Nespresso just prior to the showdown, so Amos was in a hyper-exhilarated state of mind over the upcoming challenge. Carmalita won the coin toss and began:

'Bobby Bobby hi-rollin, Ruby Ruby stone-throwin, Re Rye Ro Ruby, Tuesday'

Her lyrics immediately made Amos think of the 27 Club, and it inspired his response:

'Janice Janice mo than uth, Bobbi Bobbi mo-mobbie, Bee Bye Bo Bobbi, McGee'

Carmalita, seeing that Amos had picked up on the theme and realizing that he had sunk back into his lisping, thought she would try to trick him by using the power of suggestion, and threw in a name she hoped would lead him into a disastrous error:

'Jimi Jimi too thinny, Foxy Foxy mo-moxey, Fee Fi Fo Foxy, Lady'

Amos fired back, again playing off Carmalita's theme:

'Jimmy Jimmy too thkinny, Crawlin Crawlin mo-jo'in, Cree Cry Crow Crawlin, King Thnake'

Carmalita, not exactly sure what to do, cried out, 'BINGO', as winner of the game, claiming that Amos used the letter "s" in the words "us", "skinny", and "snake".

Amos, who was still in shock that he made any reference to the word snake, given what Abe had done to Mobie, disputed her claim. As much as he tried to explain that the words were spelled with "th" and not "s", he just wasn't able to get his tongue to specify the difference.

The crowd was roaring and wanted a winner declared. As some were supporting Carmalita and others supporting Amos, Abe brought out an Applause-o-Meter to decide the winner. When Abe asked who in the crowd supported Carmalita, a thunderous ovation erupted. He then asked who supported

Amos, and he received a smattering of feeble applause.

Abe was about to declare Carmalita the winner, but Amos objected, saying that the process was unfair because his supporters were unable to clap as enthusiastically as Carmalita's because of their hunchbacked condition, which was restricting their arm movements.

The crowd was roaring "CARMIE, CARMIE, CARMIE", so Abe had to reject Amos' protest and declared Carmalita the winner.

Amos decided to launch a lawsuit in the Supercilious Court against Abe, claiming defamation of character by "discrimination of pronunciation". The lawsuit failed abjectly; the court having consulted every thesaurus available on Google to confirm the correct spellings.

***

Amos was seeking revenge and harped on ad nauseum about the potential for voter fraud at the ballot boxes in the upcoming election. He proposed to Carmalita that they hold the vote based on crowd cheering response instead of clapping or balloting. Carmalita, inspired by her recent success, agreed to have citizens at the polling stations face-off in cheering sessions.

Full-sized cut-outs of each candidate were put up in every polling station, with a gong placed in front of each one. The rule of the election was that whoever received the least amount of cheering according to the Cheer-o-Meter would get gonged and declared the loser.

Knowing it would severely piss Amos off, Carmalita enlisted thousands of Mean Gene the Dancing Machine impersonators to support her at each of the polling stations. The crowds, who loved Gene as much as they had loved Mobie, enthusiastically cheered Carmalita on, who won the election by a cheerslide.

***

Amos claimed voter intimidation at the polling places by the Mean Gene team and launched a lawsuit for a recount, but the judges reminded him that there were no ballots to re-count, so the results stood as valid.

He considered trying to invoke Marital Law, but his most trusted advisor, poor old Rudy "Red Dress" Fool-yer-auntie (who most agreed had no future, and probably no past either), reminded him that marrying his mother was only allowed in the Great Territory of Ewe-Taw.

Bitching and whining on-and-on about voter fraud, including rigged Cheer-o-Meters and child ventriloquists lurking outside the polling places casting their cheers inside in support of Carmalita, Amos filed one lawsuit after another. Sixty-two in fact, which went all the way up to the Supercilious Court. With a bevy of expert lawyers to support his claims, it wasn't a cheap proposition. Following the series of losses, sixty-two to zip, Amos' lawyers led him through the bankruptcy proceeding, and then bolted straight to their own banks, peeling off every last penny Amos had.

After the heartbreak of their political and financial losses, Amos, Abe, and Allbliss, dejected and totally discredited, noticed what appeared to be a bad moon rising out of the east as they entered the local retro café. They took up counter stools over by the coolerator and ordered TV dinners and ginger ale. They looked about in confusion, with everyone up dancing and singing along to the music while watching the analysis of the final court decisions on See-An-End cable news network on the big screen TV. The star hosts, Beowulf's sister and Fake Rapper, were absolutely gleeful in their coverage of the Breaking News, alternatively taking turns bellowing out "YOU'RE FIRED"! YOU'RE FIRED! while laughing and giggling uncontrollably.

Abe and Allbliss were too unawares to notice that, in a strange twist of irony, someone had selected the number one hit of the week on the jukebox by a band who was turning out one chart topper after another, See-See-Arrgh! But Amos wasn't. He boiled at every word in the lyrics.

♫ We heard…some sad moans and cryin
We heard…double each dreary day
He made…us quake and he was frightnin
We heard…sad rhymes every day ♫

♫ He didn't slow down, that's right
His sound did steal the light
He…was a baboon full of lies ♫

♫ We feared…his ball and chain was rolling
He thought…he'd bend us at high noon
We got…the shivers when he was blowin
We feared…he'd double-down on all his spewin ♫

♫ He tried to mow us down in the fight
He was the clown who led the right
He…was a cartoon in life-size ♫

♫ Mayhaps…we thought we all were brothers
Wake up…lots did believe his lies
We couldn't…be further from together
We had…to rise when he lied his lies ♫

♫ We slowed him down, that's right
Kicked him out of town last night
He…was just another goon in disguise ♫

Amos waited for the humiliation to take root and sneered as he looked over at Abe. Wondering where his bus driver was, he backhanded him off the stool. He looked down at him on the floor and bellowed out, 'Ye kin be proud o yerself now, ya stinky little furball. Ya managed to accomplish two things in yer sorry excuse fer a life – turnin Allbliss into a superstar, and makin me look like an idiot, *again!*'

THE END
(mayhaps)

Kevin Clarke

Kevin Clarke is from Saint John, New Brunswick, Canada. He has lived in Alberta and Nova Scotia and is now retired and living in southern Spain. He has four children and two grandchildren in his blended family.
He has traveled extensively throughout North America and Europe and is partial to warm weather, having spent many years working outside in the harsh Alberta winters.

Kevin prefers his new life on foot, rather than by car, and spending time with his wife and their young dog, socializing with friends, and going to the beach. He recently formed a local writer's group and has several friends helping him in the challenge of learning to speak Spanish.

A collection of stories from his time as a rental property owner are contained in his memoir 'So, You Want To Be A Landlord, Eh?, which is available on Amazon.

He is in the editing process of his next novel, tentatively titled 'A Shaken Raven' which he hopes to complete in early 2023.

Kevin never once in his life thought he'd be a writer, so this is proof positive of the unexpected (some might say 'bizarre') effect a nine-week pandemic lockdown can have on a person.

Kindly offer a review of your reading experience on Amazon.

ARTISTS AND SONG CREDITS

CHAPTER	TITLE	ARTIST / BAND	SONG
	Prologue	Bob Dylan	Everything Is Broken
3	Salvation	Willie Nelson	On The Road Again
4	Hallelujah	Johnnie Cash	May The Circle (Be Unbroken)
5	The House of the Holy	Led Zepplin	Whole Lotta Love
		Queen	Fat Bottom Girls
6	The House of Holy Smokes	Bob Seger	Khatmandu
7	You Gotta Know When to Hold em	Hall & Oates	I Can't Go For That (No Can Do)
8	Nazareth	The Band	The Weight
9	Deliverance	Eric Clapton	Tulsa Time
10	Amos Meets His Pappy	The Who	Who Are You
12	Carmalita Moves on Up	ABBA	Mama Mia
13	Abe Skates on Thin Ice	Frankie Valli	Sherry
14	10th Avenue Freeze-Out	Paul Simon	50 Ways to Leave Your Lover
		The Eagles	Take It Easy
15	Amos Gets His Groove On	Pink Floyd	Money
16	Theo Gets Voted Off the Island	The Eagles	Already Gone
17	Resurrection	Elton John	Daniel
18	Thank You, Thank You Very Much	Elvis	It's Now or Never
19	Revelations	ZZ Top	Sharp Dressed Man
20	The Rainbow House gets New Tenants	Lynyrd Skynyrd	Sweet Home Alabama
21	A Very Dark Horse	Elvis Presley	Jailhouse Rock
		The Rolling Stones	Sympathy For The Devil
22	A House Divided	Tom Petty	I Won't Back Down
23	Amos Forms an Alliance	Loggins & Messina	Your Mama Don't Dance
		Elvis Presley	Blue Suede Shoes
24	A Dirty Deed, Done for Keeps	Bartok Soundtrack	Bartok the Magnificent
		The Doors	Crawling King Snake
		Dobie Gray	Drift Away
25	Exit Stage Left	Johnny Cash	Folsom Prison Blues
26	A Surprising Encounter	Aerosmith	Walk This Way
		Prince	Raspberry Beret
27	Amos Ties the Knot	The Clash	Should I Stay or Should I Go
28	The Devil Went Down To.....Taxless	Johnny Paycheck	Take This Job And Shove It
		Tom Petty	Refugee
29	Makin Hay	The Knack	My Sharona
30	Theo has a Brain Cramp	Billy Joel	You May Be Right
31	Alone Again, Naturally	Kenny Rogers	Lucille
32	The Pestilence	Don McLean	American Pie
33	Exodus	The Bee Gees	Stayin Alive
35	Revolution	The Beatles	Revolution
		Bill Withers	Ain't No Sunshine
36	The Ten Truths of Temerity	Billy Joel	You May Be Right
37	Altarin' Amos	Chuck Berry	You Never Can Tell
38	Amos Amalgamates the South	The Doors	Light My Fire
39	An Asian Virus - Part 1	Blue Oyster Cult	Don't Fear the Reaper
40	Amos Masks Up - NOT!	Lady Gaga	Poker Face
41	An Asian Virus - Part 2	Neil Diamond	Cracklin' Rosie
42	The Wheels on the Bus go Round and Round	Stevie Wonder	Superstition
		The Bee Gees	Stayin Alive
43	A Battle Cry for Amos	Queen	Medley
44	The Greatest Show on Earth	The Searchers	Love Potion Number Nine
		Eminem	Without Me
		Queen	Medley
		AC-DC	Dirty Deeds
		Michael Jackson	Beat It
45	Thenarcissist.dee-jay-tee/yourefired!	CCR	Bad Moon Rising

Printed in Poland
by Amazon Fulfillment
Poland Sp. z o.o., Wrocław

92705947R00132